CLOUD PICTURES

A Book To Read When You
Feel Life Isn't Worth Living

Martha Mud

ISBN: 979 8 84342 853 2

Independently published
www.stevenashford.co.uk

For Kevin

CLOUD PICTURES

PROLOGUE

Martha Mud jumped backwards from Suicide Bridge. She lay on the wind, but it didn't break her fall. Through her streaming hair she could see her brother staring down at her. Behind him – beyond him – the sky was a blue sheet of paper; a poem of white clouds.

Much later, when she decided to write everything down in a book – this book – she changed her name. The counsellor they gave her thought that by changing her name, and telling the story as if it had happened to someone else, she was trying to pretend it *had* happened to someone else. *You're not owning it,* her counsellor had said. Martha didn't agree with this. She wasn't pretending. And anyway, after everything that happened, she didn't need a counsellor.

Martha Mud jumped backwards from Suicide Bridge, and then she fell for a long, long time.

She hadn't meant to jump. Or rather, she *had*

meant to jump, but only to save her brother. *Look!* she was trying to tell him. *Look how crazy it is to even* think *of jumping! Look what happens when you do!*

And it was done in a moment. An impulse. She was too scared and despairing to reason it clearly. But once it was done, she couldn't take it back.

No-one survives jumping from Suicide Bridge.

This wasn't what she was thinking as she fell, although it had definitely been one of the many things she'd been thinking before she jumped.

Will it hurt?

I don't want to die!

Not these, either.

As her brother's face became a blur and then vanished, what she was thinking, was:

Those clouds are beautiful.

PART ONE

1

Martha was standing in her bedroom, by her bed. This was the same bedroom she had had since she was three years old; she could remember no other. She knew what clothes she would find if she opened the wardrobe, and looking at her bed, she recognised the chocolate stain on the quilt cover that had never quite come out. The books on the bookshelf, the framed photograph of her father on her bedside table, the half done homework open on her desk: all was as she knew it should be.

Martha couldn't remember why she was standing there, however. She couldn't remember entering her bedroom. She couldn't remember what she might have been doing before she entered.

She went over to the window and looked out. There was the steep street she'd once broken her big toe on, coming off her scooter. Opposite was the scaffolding on number 30's new porch. There were no builders, though, and no van in the drive. There were no cars anywhere, and no people, either.

Martha went to her closed bedroom door and listened. The house was silent. Her hand went to the door handle, but she didn't turn it. For a reason that she couldn't name, she was afraid.

She sat down on her bed.

Martha's mum was often exactly like this, she realised suddenly: vague, and anxious, and unsure of why she had come to whichever room of the house Martha would find her standing in. She would nibble her fingers and laugh when Martha asked her. Pretend she was busy. Make something up.

Yesterday had been school, and the day before that, and the day before that. But no – how could she have forgotten? – yesterday had been a weekend, and Martha had gone with her friend to the cinema. A superhero blockbuster that neither of them had enjoyed particularly, but that everyone else had seen and so they went, and then they'd laughed about that minor character's dodgy fake-Brit accent over milkshakes afterwards.

Except hadn't that been more like a month ago?

Oh, dear. That had been a year ago. Last

summer, her friend had moved to Wales.

Martha bit her lip and closed her eyes.

She had been on the bridge with her brother. Her brother had delivered some terrible news, about his life and how it had suddenly bent apart and broken. Her brother had talked about jumping. No way through it but out. No way out of it but down.

And then he'd jumped.

No.

Martha had jumped instead.

Martha had jumped for him.

What had happened after?

She remembered falling. She couldn't remember landing.

She opened her eyes and looked at the alarm clock next to the photograph on her bedside table. It read *00:00:00,* like a factory re-set.

Was this an end, or a beginning?

She lay back on her bed and looked towards the ceiling, but her bedroom had no ceiling. Framed by four walls was a blank square of sky.

Then Martha began falling upwards.

2

This is the hardest part to piece together, and the hardest part to describe clearly. She plummeted into a wide, soft purple without cloud or horizon. She sensed she was falling faster and faster, although there was no resistance to this movement. She only felt a pressure in her chest that seemed to be pulling her up, and up, and up.

Martha had had dreams before of falling – she supposes everyone has – where there was always a split second of thinking, *Here I go, this is it* – an instant of realising that this was a point of no return, that it was her alone falling and that no-one would catch her – followed immediately by an enormous, heart-stopping dread that yanked her out of sleep.

Falling from the bridge hadn't felt like that, and neither did this.

She had left her bed as gently as a feather, and had entered the sky like she might have entered a warm bath. But now she was in it, she knew there was something beyond it; and it was partly this knowledge that was lifting her with increasing velocity towards – what?

Something that drew her heart like a magnet. Something that she did not want to want: not yet. She felt herself starting to panic.

And there were voices.

Too soon.

Push her back.

Push her on. Push her up.

She won't.

Push her back.

If Martha felt not the slightest breeze in her headlong passage through this sky, then the voices were gale and whirlwind, typhoon and hurricane: a raging anemology of tug and counter-tug, batter and blast. And the pressure in her chest was consuming her. Whatever was lifting her up desired her, and expected its desire to be returned.

NO! screamed Martha.

The pressure eased. The panic eased. Hanging, she stopped.

The voices continued.

Push her back.

She won't. She can't.

She can't stay here!

She must.

She can't.

Leave her.

Leave her.

Leave her.

While her heart was lifting her upwards, Martha hadn't had time to pay attention to these voices. Now she knew she would rise no further, the voices filled her with helplessness and confusion. The beings to whom they belonged were a part of this strange sky, as she was not.

What will become of her?
Leave her. Not our problem.
Not our business.
Let her drift.
Not our problem.
What will become of her?

Martha was very used to feeling alone. Her brother, so much older than her, had wandered away into life with hardly a backward glance, until the day he'd suddenly needed her. Her mother had been wandering away into somewhere opposed to life, somewhere numb and silent and dark, since as long as Martha could remember. Her dad had simply left.

Now, though, Martha knew herself to be more completely alone than she'd thought it was possible to be, and the realisation terrified her.

The voices had all whirled away. The sky in which she hung was a lilac desert.

No. Two voices remained.

I will help her.
None of your business.
I will help her.
How? You can't.
I will.

Then there was silence. Martha floated, neither rising nor falling. The warm bath of this sky was growing tepid; she could feel her heart cooling. How tiny she was, and how fragile! This wasn't a place she belonged in.

Martha sensed a presence, very close to her.

A boy appeared.

3

Martha still felt as if she were spread out on her back, although there was no ground below her, or moon or stars in the opposite direction, or yearning pull in her chest, to tell her she was right. But if she really was on her back, then the boy was directly above her, just beyond her reach. He was staring down at her.

Then he seemed to slide around and sideways, until it felt like Martha was lying on a bed, and the boy was standing patiently beside her.

Martha turned her head to him, and stared back.

He looked about eight or nine years old. He was covered in something white, or silver, that seemed to flicker over his body in never ending motion. It was dazzling. Martha couldn't tell if it was feathers, or clothing, or even some kind of pelt. His eyes were like a baby's eyes. They were the eyes of something that must have arrived where it now was from an unimaginable distance.

The boy spoke.

"You're stuck," he said.

And then he laughed.

Since waking in her bedroom – if waking was what it was – Martha hadn't tried her voice to see if it still worked. She really wasn't sure if it would.

"Where am I?" she said.

It did work, but it sounded remote and thin, as if it didn't quite belong to her.

"This is Air," said the boy.

His own voice was jocund and careless. Breezy. The sound it made was quick and bright.

"What am I supposed to do?" she said. "Where do I go?"

As if she was some clueless first-year kid at a new school.

"You're stuck," repeated the boy. He smiled at her. "Up, or back. There are only two directions. You're stuck because you can't choose."

Martha had to think about this for quite a while.

"I jumped off a bridge," she said. "It was pretty high up. Am I dead?"

"No," said the boy. "It's as I said. You need to choose."

"Who are you?" asked Martha.

His laugh was like a bagful of jingling coins. His teeth were almost too bright to look at.

"I don't have a name," he said. "Beings with names can be called, and I have no desire to be called."

"You said you'd help me," Martha pleaded.

"In the face of wise advice. And not knowing

how to help. But yes. I will try."

Martha hung, and the boy slid round again; except this time it felt as if Martha were sliding too, and they wound up face to face once more, but somehow, both of them, *upright.*

"You can't stay here for too much longer," he said. "You're too high up. Let me move you somewhere else."

"Move me?"

"You can't move on your own. But let me show you Air," he said. "Where you are."

4

Martha Mud's father's name was Lionel. Her mother still spoke about him, sometimes, and when she did, her eyes always tried to light up: as if they felt they wanted to, but couldn't quite.

Martha never talked about him at all, not to anyone.

The Lionel Martha had known was tall and lanky, with his Mr Tickle limbs always in motion: gesturing, waving, pointing. Posturing, quite often. Flailing. His eyes were blue and his stubble was red. A doggy, devastating smile. A voice with an accent that her mother didn't share, but that Martha could still mimic, if she wanted to.

Martha's dad had gone touring his motorbike in Australia and had never come back.

He'd sent letters from that other side of the world, which the eight year old Martha could stumblingly read. She still had them. She kept them in a box in the bottom of her wardrobe, with doodles and half-started diaries and old birthday cards.

Only a couple of these cards were from

Lionel.

The letters were long, and carefully, almost childishly handwritten, at the start of them anyway. (By the end, they were often scrawled and sentimental, and occasionally wild.) They told of life in the desert racing bikes. They were boastful and endearing, and always they said *Martha, Martha, Martha* in nearly every line.

We saw a herd of wallabies, Martha, jumping all over the place, right by the track! You'd have loved them! I was scared they'd dive under my wheels – I didn't know if I was racing wallabies or bikes!

Martha still wasn't sure if wallabies really came in herds, or in something else.

It's so hot in this hotel room, you wouldn't believe it. I think the air conditioning's on the blink. I hope you can read this, Martha darling, because it looks like there's more sweat than biro on this piece of paper. And it's supposed to be the beginning of autumn over here!

I'm imagining you scoffing Easter eggs. Did your mum hide them in the garden for you? Sorry. That should have been my job, shouldn't it?

And:

I got talking to this guy from Kentucky and he says the scene in the States is crazy. I'm thinking of heading over there, just to check it out. So I might be gone for a little while longer. I don't know yet. I'll write and tell you.

But he never had.

Eight year old memories? A funfair, and

standing in line for a ride with gigantic tattooed women painted across its sides, and a board with lines and numbers on it propped up by the gate. A height restriction. Martha had stood against it, and she could tell by the attendant's stony expression that she wasn't tall enough. But then her dad had flashed that game-over grin of his, and the look of the attendant changed instantly.

"It's only an inch. Just a couple of fingers. She's my baby girl. I'll guard her with my life."

And on they'd gone.

Getting that gleaming scooter for her sixth birthday; tearing the paper off ("It was such a pain in the bum to wrap, Martha, I'll tell you!"), nearly wetting herself with happiness. He'd helped her learn to ride it, not down their steep hill to start with, they'd taken it to the park. When she'd got confident with it, he'd run alongside her, those lean legs pumping. Once, he'd got his bike out and they'd had a jokey kind of race. She remembers the tang of petrol in her nose; the snarl of his engine right at her back, as if she was being chased by a beast.

Lionel.

He'd let her win, of course. But she'd known all along how silly it was. A scooter against a motorbike?!

There were other memories. Silent breakfasts: her dad looking agitated and angry, her mum with sleepless moons of black beneath her eyes.

Sometimes, yelling from their bedroom in the middle of the night.

I miss you so much my darling Martha, I can't stand not being with you, I've decided I'm coming home, I'm catching the first plane out of here, right after this next one...

That was the end of the last letter Martha's dad wrote – a scribbled postscript – after his final *I love you forever* goodbyes.

5

"In Air, Everywhere is Anywhere," said the boy.

"I don't know what you mean," said Martha.

"I mean this."

Martha gasped.

The sky was no longer purple, it was blue, and fluffy clouds floated under her feet. Martha had never been in an aeroplane, but this was what she imagined it must be like. Between the drifting edges of the clouds, she thought she could glimpse the greens and browns of land, far below her.

What land? What country was that? She stared and stared.

"Further up – further in – they say that Anywhere is Everywhere. Water. Fire. Not places such as I could be in."

The boy was right next to her, and Martha looked hard at him. It was difficult to look hard at him.

"Are you an angel?" she said.

The boy winced.

"We don't speak of angels." And then he laughed again, like silver bells pealing. "And yet you are higher than angels, if you only knew it. You could go to the place where Anywhere is Everywhere. You belong there. If you only knew it."

Martha looked away from him, back to the clouds. The boy's words didn't make much sense to her; or if they did, it was a sense that she mustn't take hold of: not yet. She resisted it.

"Come," he said.

Now Martha felt herself descending with him, into the heart of a cloud fat as whipped cream. She expected cold and discomforting damp, expected the billowing surface of it to wrap around her ankles and suck her in, but what she experienced wasn't physical at all.

"It's alive!" she gasped.

"There is nothing not alive," said the boy.

The cloud was a whirling of ideas and images and emotions. Hope, and desire, and delight. Hopeless regret, twisting and turning. Love, and loathing, and everything in between. She saw a tree in summer, chockfull of sparrows. A snowman wearing a straw hat. A box of chocolates tied with a red ribbon. A taxi carrying someone precious, someone irreplaceable, disappearing into distance.

They were out of the cloud. They were below it, and Martha watched its towering splendour topple, and shift, and melt.

"It was a person," she said. "It was an old man. I felt him. All of him."

She was breathless with what the cloud had revealed to her.

"We make them," said the boy. "We make them out of what you give to us."

"He was so sad," said Martha. "He was so happy." She was awestruck by the depth of what she'd felt. "But where is he now?"

"He's gone," said the boy. "Further up. Further in."

The cloud above them wasn't the same cloud any longer. The intricate architecture of a moment before had changed to something else.

"I don't understand," said Martha, and she felt a weight of grief settle down over her shoulders.

"It was a life," said the boy. "We fashion clouds from them. All of your humanness winds up here. Your hate. Your mendacity. Your cruelty. Storms and thunderheads and hurricanes. The task is endless."

"But that cloud was...beautiful," said Martha.

"It was," agreed the boy.

"But now it's gone. It didn't last."

"Nothing in Earth or in Air lasts," said the boy. "Surely everyone knows that. But let me show you something else."

6

When Martha Mud tried to describe all this to her counsellor, you can imagine she made a mess of it. The words wouldn't come out right, and she kept forgetting to mention things and muddling up their order. And it was hard enough just to get started, because even if she somehow managed to communicate what had happened to her, Martha felt sure her counsellor would never believe her. (What right-thinking person, let alone a mental health care professional, would believe a story like *that?*) So she stammered and stumbled her way through it, and her counsellor listened attentively, and asked tactful questions in some of the right places, because that was her job, and she seemed to be pretty good at it. But Martha struggled to make much sense of her story, and struggled to imagine she was really being heard.

Here's a typical bit of conversation. Judge for yourself if Martha did a good job of explaining, or if her counsellor – let's call her Mary – came anywhere near understanding it.

"So you were somewhere up in the sky,

Martha?"

"We were in Air."

"You saw clouds. You saw the earth below you."

"They looked like clouds, but they weren't. They were people. The stories of people."

"Are you saying that clouds are really... That they're made..."

"No. Not Earth clouds. Not the clouds you can see out the window. Those are just clouds. The Earth part of clouds. We were in Air."

"So how about the land you say you saw, the greens and browns. Could you have gone down to it? Could you have come back down to earth again?"

"Air and Earth overlap. I went to Earth loads of times. But I was always still in Air."

"Do you mean you were flying?"

"No! How could I have been flying? Aeroplanes fly. Birds fly. I was in *Air!*"

Do you see what Martha means?

When Mary suggested she write it down instead, Martha knew at once that this was the right thing to try. Now she found she could tell her story as slowly and carefully as she needed to, and that she could go back and edit when her words didn't sound right, which was incredibly often. A lot of the time, the events and things and feelings she was trying to describe were so fantastic that she found herself using words she wouldn't have dreamed of using until they wound up on the page.

Words. Martha came to love words. She started actually enjoying using a dictionary. And she tried incredibly hard to use these words in a way that would give the best idea of what had happened to her. The style she ended up writing in was miles and miles away from how she'd tried to tell the story to her counsellor, and whether this other way of telling it works any better, Martha still has no idea; but at least she has the satisfaction of knowing that the words she ended up choosing were the best ones she could find, and that if Mary still doesn't believe her story, at least she's told it in the most truthful way she can think of.

But anyway (because all of this is part of the story, too): when Martha had been trying and failing to explain the old man's cloud for quite a while, Mary suddenly came out with:

"These pictures you saw. Can you tell me more about them?"

"There were a million of them. But they were more than just pictures. They were so hard to grasp, though. It all happened in a flash."

"A tree full of sparrows. A box of chocolates."

"They were memories. It was what the old man remembered. What came back to him."

"And a taxi? You said it was disappearing?"

"Yes. Driving off, down the road."

"Do you know who was in the taxi?"

"It was the old man's father, when the old man was just a boy. The father was in uniform. He was being taken to the train station. He was going to the war."

"The war?"

"Maybe it was the Second World War. Maybe it was another one. I don't know. But he never came back."

Mary went quiet then, and I looked at her. Her lips were pressed together and trembling, as if she had too many things to say for her to choose from. I could see a little buzz of excitement building in her that she was trying to hold down.

"Your own father, Martha. Do you think that maybe…?"

"What do you mean?" I said.

"You've told me that your father left when you were eight. Do you have a memory of him going? Did he leave in a taxi, perhaps? I'm sorry. I know it's a leading question."

"My dad never took taxis," I said. "He had his motorbike."

Another silence, and then Mary couldn't help grinning.

"This taxi," she said. "The cloud taxi. Was it any particular colour?"

"It was black," I said.

"It wasn't yellow?" said Mary. "A big, yellow taxi?"

I must have looked at her with complete incomprehension, and then she explained. I hadn't ever heard of Joni Mitchell, or heard the song about a taxi taking away her old man, although actually (I looked it up) it wasn't her father but her boyfriend she was singing about.

Big Yellow Taxi by Joni Mitchell. It's good. Dear reader, check it out.

After that – as I kept telling this story – I could see that Mary felt completely out of her depth, and that she could see that I saw. She was a counsellor, not a psychoanalyst. But amazingly, the result of her feeling out of her depth was that she settled into herself, and listened. Really listened. Even when my telling got horribly confused and incompetent.

And look: I've started using the first person. I'm writing "I" instead of "Martha".

But don't get confused, dear reader. As I told you right at the start, the girl putting these words down is no longer Martha Mud.

This story happened to someone else.

7

The sky and clouds were both gone. Martha recognised at once a hospital ward, because she'd seen a hundred of them on television: beds, and machines, and drips, and silent blue-uniformed nurses. Except she knew straight away that this was real, not fictional. For a start, nothing was happening. Nothing was about to happen, either – nothing important, nothing scripted – but still, anything at all *might* happen. A terrible intensity of *nowness* filled the room.

The boy was with her. They were hovering near the ceiling. A bed was below them.

"Look," said the boy.

A girl lay on the bed. Beneath the mask that was strapped over her mouth and nose, terrible bruises puffed up her face out of all recognition. One leg, in plaster, jutted out of the sheets. Machines blinked by her side, and tubes were taped to her arms.

"Here is your body," said the boy.

Martha stared. Yes, she could see now that the thing on the bed might well once have belonged to her. It was about the right size, and the hair colour was the right kind of brown. But Martha felt no connection. She glanced at the next bed along and at the man who lay in it. A stranger.

"You're not tethered," said the boy.

"Tethered?"

"It won't draw you back. It isn't even breathing."

Not breathing. The mask was a respirator. So this is it, she thought. She felt curiously blank. That's my body, and I really did fall. She experienced a momentary gratitude that she hadn't been conscious, that the awful injuries sustained by the girl on this bed hadn't been hers to deal with, hers to feel. And then the blankness returned.

The boy was speaking.

"You're free to choose. But you must choose."

"Go back," said Martha, seeing what this meant.

"Or go forward," said the boy.

And now Martha remembered rising into that purple sky – how long ago had it been? – not very long ago, surely, but it felt like a lifetime – and how she'd rebelled against the furious tugging of her heart. Refusing that summons had hurt as much as anything, and even the memory of it stung her. Yet her will to refuse – the necessity of refusing – had been even stronger.

But why? For what?

This body on the bed wasn't her. Martha

hadn't the tiniest wish to return to it. Looking at its pale skin and slouching limbs, Martha felt nothing but a small, detached kind of sympathy for it.

"What if I choose neither?" she said quietly.

The boy shrugged. His eyes were diamond-cold.

"Untethered, you'll drift. You'll wander. Air is wide. But you'll have no say in it."

Martha thought about this. She tried to find a desire for such an existence inside her, unimaginable as it was.

"I don't know," she said.

But the boy hadn't finished.

"The winds of Air will push and pull you, and for a time, perhaps you'll be content. Air is your element just as much as Earth. But Air alone will slowly make you threadbare. Its winds will whistle through you. Your substance will shred and fade, until there's nothing of you left."

"No," Martha said.

"I didn't make the rules."

"You said you'd help me."

"I'm trying to help you now. But this is as much as I can do, and far more than I should be doing. Show you. Tell you. I can't help you choose."

"I can't choose."

And it was only then, as Martha contemplated the body of the girl below her and the seemingly impossible decision she was now supposed to make, that she experienced an utter, blinding panic. She stretched out her arm. It was clothed in her blue denim jacket, the jacket she'd been wearing when she jumped from Suicide Bridge. She could see fingers poking from the jacket cuffs, and surely these fingers were hers? But this other girl below her had fingers of her own. Martha could see them clearly above the sheets, bruised and bandaged as they were.

"Take me back," she told the boy.

"Back?"

"To the clouds. Now. Take me Anywhere."

The hospital ward vanished. They were skimming across the tops of white-crested waves. Seagulls wove around them.

"What am I?" she said.

The boy stared at her.

Martha looked down at herself. School shoes. Tights. Skirt and jacket. What was underneath them? She tried with all her might to sense the body she was in: to feel what it ought to be feeling. The sea air rushing past her face and blowing back her hair; the salty taste of it; the heart below her ribs, which should have been hammering like crazy with the effort it seemed to be taking.

For a moment, she thought she might have felt something. Then all sensation left her.

She looked down again, and her clothes had

vanished. She was naked.

Then she watched in disbelief as her skin grew insubstantial, until all that was left were the grey waters of the ocean roiling beneath her.

"What do you see?" she demanded. "Look at me! What do you see?"

Still staring, the boy said:

"I see what you are. I see a soul."

8

Martha's mum's name was Joan. She'd claimed she'd always hated it. Dull as dishwater, she'd said.

Lionel had always disagreed, loudly and loquaciously. But just think what company you're keeping! he'd said. Joan Crawford. Joan Collins. Joan Armatrading. Joan Jett.

Years later – remembering her father naming names, but not remembering exactly what names they'd been – Martha googled *Joan* and got the names you've just read. And her father had been right, if these were actually the names he'd mentioned: it really was good company her mum had been keeping. They were strong, talented, spirited women.

Martha's mum, when Martha jumped, was none of these things. She was dull through and through, but not like dishwater, the scintillating soap-bubble colours of which Martha came to know intimately, after Lionel left. Joan was dull like pasta with no pesto. Like a rainy day in Margate. Like a tune heard through earmuffs. The strength, the talent, the spirit, had all leaked out.

When it had been the four of them – except Martha's brother had always been a little distant, a little apart from them – Joan had sparkled. That's what the eight year old Martha still remembered: a dazzling, dancing, fiery chatterbox, readier to sing than to snap, although she could do either with a will; and tea-times were a non-stop, razor-tongued crossfire of banter: the South London mum, the Irish dad.

Those silent, edgy breakfasts had only started gradually, and Martha never knew what her parents had been arguing about. But then Lionel would leave for work, and perhaps he wouldn't be back for tea that night anyway, and by the time Martha came home from school, Joan would be herself again, zesty and alive.

Lionel's job was in civil construction. He had licences for everything, diggers, forklifts, HGVs, although how he could ever have throttled back his daredevil motorbike temperament to drive such lumbering beasts, Martha couldn't guess. His working week was piecemeal, so actually, breakfasts and tea-times with everyone together weren't regular events. He'd work weekends, quite often, or nights; or sometimes he'd be away for several days, building a bridge in Southsea, a bypass in Faversham. Martha didn't particularly think to miss him when he was gone. It was how life was, she couldn't imagine it being different; and of course, she knew he'd always be back.

Joan missed him. Martha thinks now that

Joan missed him: missed him constantly. Perhaps that was because Joan *could* imagine different. But Martha's only guessing.

Martha watched her mum begin to fade as soon as Lionel left for Australia. No: even before he left. It was a huge thing, a chance in a lifetime, and Lionel would brag and enthuse and gabble about it wildly, while Martha's mum just went quiet. Lionel was jacking in his job and going pro. He'd been talent-spotted by an Aussie scout – a three month tour, just a try-out, really – but if he placed consistently, there ought to be big bucks in it. I'll fly you all out, first class! claimed Lionel. I'll buy you the moon, baby daughter!

Motocross. Lionel's obsession. Joan went to see him race often, but Martha was never allowed to, however much she pleaded. She's too young, Joan said. Martha thinks now that what her mum meant was: She's too young to see you hurt yourself, or kill yourself. Which was only sensible parenting, although she couldn't understand it then.

Martha's brother never went, either. Why would he want to see his step-dad race motorbikes? Usually, he ended up babysitting.

Once Lionel was in Australia, while Martha got letters, what did her mother get? Martha doesn't know. Martha doesn't know why her dad never emailed or skyped, or even just called, although she could imagine the excuses. The time difference; out here in the sticks, there's just no connection; you know me and technology (Lionel did petrol, but was hopeless with electric).

Martha still treasures those letters. She thinks it wonderful that her dad bothered to write and seal and stamp such old-fashioned assurances of love. She's incredibly grateful for them; even while a little voice inside her is saying that maybe Lionel wrote her letters because he was already wondering if they'd be the last piece of him she'd have.

When the three months were over – more than over, Martha was already thinking about her ninth birthday – Joan took her and her brother to the seaside. Whitstable. A sunny summer's day, and they'd swum, and her brother had wolfed raw oysters and pretended he liked them, and after lunch at a beach pub, sat outside on wooden benches with a coke and a pint and a spritzer, Joan had told them Lionel wasn't coming home again. Not ever. That he was now in America and had found someone else.

Martha can still see her mum's face as it was that day. She can see it turned out towards the waves, the wind blowing her hair from under her sunhat, her cheeks pink, her eyes dry but shining a bit too brightly. Because looking back, it seems to Martha that that was her mum's goodbye, too. This is the last you'll see of me, that face says. I'm not coming back, either. Farewell, my daughter.

9

"Can I stop you?" Mary said.

We were sitting in her room at the CAMHS unit. (That's "Child and Adolescent Mental Health Service", in case you don't know; but I bet a lot of you do.) I'd been trying to find words for the impossible for the last half an hour. It was exhausting.

"You say you saw yourself lying in a bed."

"Yes."

"There's an extensive literature of people having similar... *experiences*. Similar to the ones you've been describing, I mean. Out of body experiences."

I could tell Mary had nearly said *hallucinations*. I could tell she'd really wanted to say it, and regretted that she hadn't felt able to.

"You suffered a severe head trauma. You'd stopped breathing. They had to put you on a respirator. This all really happened, Martha, just as you say you saw it."

I didn't feel there was anything I needed to add to that.

"Consciousness is something miraculous. It's something we still don't really understand. What's really going on inside coma patients..."

She left this hanging, but I wasn't about to let her get away with it.

"I wasn't *inside,*" I said. "That's the point. That's why I was so terrified."

"Go on," she said.

"If that was my body down there on the bed, and if I wasn't part of it any more, then what was I?"

"You told me the boy gave you an answer," Mary said quietly. "A soul."

"Yes."

"And what do you think a soul is, Martha?"

When I didn't reply, after a few moments Mary said:

"You've already told me you weren't brought up in any organised religion. But would you say either of your parents are religious, in the broader sense? Have they ever talked to you about what they think happens to us when we die?"

"My mum's an atheist. I'm not sure about Lionel. He was Irish, so maybe he was brought up Catholic. But no, he never talked about it."

"Would you say *you're* religious, Martha?"

I didn't know whether to laugh at this. I watched her sitting there, my counsellor, with her kind, clever eyes, and it struck me suddenly that if she hadn't heard my story yet, how was she supposed to know what a ridiculously inadequate question she'd just asked me?

And why have I included this little part of the story? Well, I said just a few pages ago that Mary really started to listen, after the big yellow taxi gambit didn't pay off. And that was more or less true, despite her coma theories and religion confusion. But after *this* conversation, it was me who changed. Up until now, I'd been putting myself through hell trying to tell the story, and failing most of the time – I thought – and I was always just on the edge of giving up. Why bother? I kept wondering. Why waste so much time and effort trying to tell the untellable?

But there in the counselling room, I looked at Mary's completely baffled face looking back at me, and I realised suddenly that we were both in the same boat. Maybe I hadn't been doing her justice. Maybe listening truly was as difficult and time-consuming as telling truly. Mary didn't seem to know what she was doing any more than I did, and yet she obviously cared enough about me to want to understand.

Despite probably feeling that she just wasn't up to it, Mary was committed, and I had to be committed, too. Giving up wasn't an option. I just had to keep on going till I reached the end.

10

A soul.

That meant nothing to Martha whatsoever. She knew that Save Our Souls was what S.O.S was short for, morse code for *Help!* sent by sailors in storms who were about to be drowned. Well, seeing the seawater slide through her transparent limbs, she thought she knew what drowning might be like: to have the waves fill you up so entirely that there's nothing of you left. The sea is there, but you no longer are, and that's that.

The boy floated beside her, looking just about as solid and real as a being with dazzling eyes and quicksilver skin could be expected to look. In fact, Martha realised that beside the waves and the seagulls – and even more so beside the subdued, scrubbed walls of the hospital ward – the boy looked *more* than real. But did real equate to solid? If she still had her body, would he have been touchable? Somehow, Martha doubted it.

And how was she seeing him, anyway? Where, *what,* were her eyes?

"Where have I gone?" she yelped.

"Nowhere," the boy said. "You are here, with me. In Air."

"My body! My arms and legs! Just now I was wearing *clothes!*"

"No," the boy said. He seemed to consider for a moment. "Perhaps you held a memory. The memory has faded."

"How am I even speaking? What do you see when you look at me? Tell me what you see!"

The boy regarded her quizzically. Then he grinned.

"A flame," he said. "A flower. A feather."

Martha felt close to tears. Tears, she thought, falling from no eyes, and into the ocean. How can I cry without tears?

"Air is many things," the boy said. "Appearance is one of them. Here, the surface of things and the essence of things are one and the same. And yet here also, the surface of things is constantly changing, just as the clouds are constantly changing. Now, tell me: what do you see when you look at *me?*"

The boy seemed genuinely curious.

"You're a boy," said Martha. "You're too bright to look at sometimes. You're about nine years old. Whatever you're wearing – I don't even know if it's what you're wearing – but it's like…" She thought for a moment. "It's like a sparkler on Bonfire Night."

He smiled tentatively.

"Thank you," he said.

"For what?"

"For seeing me, and telling me what you make of me. I've never been seen by a soul before."

"What are you?" asked Martha, herself now genuinely curious. "If you're not a soul, and this body of a boy I'm seeing isn't real, then what are you?"

"A Being of Air," said the boy. "I am nothing else."

Martha hung beside the boy, above the ocean, for a long while. She thought about the body in the hospital that had once been hers. She tried to feel herself: all of herself: what she was, now. She tried with all her strength and concentration to discount the illusions of hands (not that), of lips and tongue (not that), of stomach and sex (not that, not that!).

She was awareness. She was what she felt. She was what she thought, however inadequate that thinking might be. She was memory. She was what she saw and what she heard.

She was what she said, too, if speaking was what she was doing: she was what the boy seemed to hear from her when she imagined making words; but no other act of will seemed possible for her.

Martha contemplated this little mote of her – what was left of her – drifting without volition or purpose. She thought about the boy's prediction (was he right?): that slowly, whatever *she* now was would grow thin and insubstantial, just like she'd watched her illusory arms and legs grow thin and insubstantial, and then disappear completely.

But the idea of this made her think of her mother, of Joan, who'd seemed to be drifting for years, and getting more and more see-through by the day.

Becoming her mother was certainly not what she wanted!

So what were her choices?

Go back: to that broken body on the bed. Whether this body had pushed her away, or whether she'd abandoned it, really didn't matter. Neither did it matter if it was broken or whole. Martha didn't want it. That was part of why she'd jumped.

Go forward: but to where and what? She remembered how it had felt for her heart to desire something so completely; for her heart to be pulled upwards by something that desired her just the same. The pull and the desire had gone, but whatever had willed her to resist must still be there inside her.

Martha searched for it.

"I want to move," she said. "I want to be able to move. Here, in Air."

"Everything moves in Air," said the boy.

"That's not what I mean. You've given me three options, but I don't choose any of them. I want to go where I want, not yanked up into something I'm not ready for. Not just pulled every which way by the wind, either. Or by you."

"I was trying to help," he said.

"And I want you to be my friend. Not my wheelchair. Not my jailor."

"What you want isn't possible."

Martha felt exasperation welling inside her. How could she explain it to him?

"You don't understand," she said. "It's not what I want. It's what I *need*."

The boy looked sorrowful and doubtful.

"You're an untethered soul. You can't break the rules."

"Why not?" asked Martha.

And all at once, she found what had stopped her upward flight: what had forced her to refuse. It was rage.

"Watch me," she said. "Just watch me."

It wasn't like walking. Using your legs meant you had to have an idea of using them, an intention of using them, and usually some notion of where you wanted them to go; and after that, they pretty much did it on their own. Martha didn't have any legs, and here, in Air, she had no way of guessing what their equivalent might be. So she started with trying to imagine a destination, and a very clear picture came up out of nowhere right away.

That was the easy bit.

The waves rose and fell below her. The boy

stayed beside her: watching, impassively, just as she'd told him to.

The boy had said that Air was her element. She imagined little fishes darting through water with a twist and a flick of their fins. But she had no fins. The wind flowed around her, and there seemed to be no part of her she could use to push against it.

Except, no: the wind didn't flow around her. How could it flow around her if she had no body?

Air flowed through her. She was part of it.

Everywhere is Anywhere. Isn't that what he'd said?

And as if by magic, Martha found herself somewhere else. She didn't feel like she'd moved at all, but that this new world of Air had simply shifted its appearance, like an optical illusion, like an Arcimboldo face.

This was the place she had willed to be: the image that had come to her.

Suicide Bridge.

But the boy was no longer with her.

11

Martha didn't really know how her brother had felt when Lionel had come into his mother's life. They hadn't ever talked about it, any more than they'd talked about how Martha had felt when Lionel left it again. But Martha's brother would have been exactly the same age. Exactly the same age.

Martha's brother's name was Mark. His own dad had died when he was two. A traffic accident. He didn't remember a single thing about him.

Martha grew up in awe of her brother. He was always doing something else that didn't include her: playing with friends she hardly knew the names of, or up to whatever with his bedroom door closed; learning to ride a bike before she'd learned to walk; coming home late from parties before she was even allowed to go out on her own to buy sweets from the cornershop.

All this sounds like she might have resented him; but it was just the opposite.

He'd always been kind to her. He had a talent for drawing, and he created elaborate and beautiful birthday cards for her – cards she kept in that box in her wardrobe – cards that ended up far out-numbering Lionel's. When she'd been younger, he'd played silly games with her on rainy afternoons, and tickled her, and given her piggyback rides. He'd never grumbled when Lionel and Joan went out and he was told to look after her.

After Lionel left for Australia, Mark's babysitting services were very rarely needed; but now, he was taking her to school on the bus, and cooking her tea when she got home again, and washing her uniform, and helping her with her homework. He'd just started college, and Martha has no idea how he found the time or the energy to pick up Joan's slack for her. Two years later, while Martha was still at Junior School, he found a job as a photographer at a local newspaper. When he got his first pay packet, he came home with flowers for Joan and a shiny, blingy bracelet for Martha. She'd worn it daily until it broke, and she'd cried and cried.

Even earning a comfortable amount – and he was making extra money in the evenings doing what he really loved, drawing pictures that he sold to various magazines – Mark had kept living at home for another three years. Martha can only think that he stuck around for so long because he felt obliged to be some kind of support for Joan. Then, just about the time that Martha was entering her own locked-bedroom phase, he moved into a flat in a neighbouring town. Martha missed him: not because they'd been spending much time together, but because now, it was just her and her mum, and that was scary, and hard.

Probably, Martha liked the idea of her big older brother better than the reality. Growing up, she'd boasted constantly about his looks, his size, his coolness to her school friends. *I'll get my brother to beat you up.* Yeah? How old's your brother? *He's nearly twenty, and he could have your whole family!*

Kids say stupid things, don't they? But Martha felt such fierce joy saying them. The idea of her brother – the Mark she thought about, and talked about – almost made up for not having a dad.

The reality was different. The reality was a tired, endlessly patient, preoccupied adult, who was happier tinkering alone in the kitchen than entertaining his sister, or trying to coax conversation out of his mum. On the bus together, Mark and Martha were usually silent. After he'd finished her bedtime story and turned out the light, Martha often heard the front door go, and footsteps on the drive.

Martha feels she never really knew her brother. Whatever problems he had, he never shared them. He'd always had an aura of privacy about him, and once Lionel was out of the picture, this aura seemed to intensify.

But how could he have opened up to a girl half his age?

And Martha's pretty sure he never opened up

to Joan, because opening up to Joan would have been like opening up to a rock.

A couple more years went by, and Martha discovered problems of her own – the kind of problems every teenager has, Martha supposes – dealing with them single-handed, sometimes well, sometimes badly. Mark came for Christmases and birthdays and the odd, flying visit, always unaccompanied. There was supposedly a girlfriend, an off-and-on crush he'd had since college, but whoever she was, she was never introduced to mum and sister.

Then there was a long period – a few months – of nothing. Martha got the odd text, *How's things little sis,* which she replied to without really replying.

Then she got the text that said, *We need to talk. Come and meet me.*

And she had. And Mark really had needed to talk. And for the first time in Martha's life, although not entirely with words, they told each other all kinds of things that needed to be said.

12

So here she was again. She was hanging just above the spot where they'd been sitting, so that if the two of them were still there, she'd have been peering over their shoulders at the drop below.

It was a disused railway viaduct. The tracks had been taken up and turned into a cycle path; the views of the Downs in the distance were hazily beautiful. "Suicide Bridge" was part of the local folklore, amongst schoolkids anyway. Martha had no idea how many people had ever actually jumped, or even if anyone had, but whatever local authority took charge of such things obviously thought that someday someone might, so they'd erected fierce metal spikes all along both sides of it. Still, if you were brave or stupid enough, you could duck the barbed wire at the end, and swing yourself round, and haul yourself along the bridge's length using hands and toes, until right at its middle there was a metal platform just wide enough to sit on. And there, you could swing your legs and contemplate the rocky gorge narrowing to a point below you.

Now she was here, Martha knew she didn't really want to be here. She'd needed to move, and a picture of the bridge had popped into her head; but what had happened in this place belonged to that smashed up body in the hospital: a body she'd said goodbye to.

She looked at the little dried up stream that snaked its way along the bottom of the gorge. It was such a long way down. She found herself wondering, with a shudder, where exactly she might have landed.

She looked up. The sky was a uniform grey. The sun had probably set, although peculiarly, in Air, you often couldn't tell. Shadows were gathering.

Where was the boy?

She'd moved, by her own will. The boy had said she couldn't, but she had, and a little thrill of triumph shook her profoundly. It wasn't a feeling Martha was used to.

But what should she do now?

Suddenly, Martha realised that someone was staring at her. It was the closest to an actual physical sensation that she'd so far had. There was someone down there at the bottom of the gorge, and as Martha watched, this figure began to rise slowly up towards her. It came closer and closer, until Martha was able to see it quite clearly.

It was a very young girl, maybe only five or six. She was waif-like, with thin little arms and legs, and a mass of tangled, curly hair that nearly hid her face. Her feet were bare. She wore a dull-coloured, short-sleeved dress that was ripped at the hem. Her eyes were very wide and very black.

"What are you doing?" asked the girl in a high, clear voice.

Martha didn't reply, and the girl just stared.

There was something slightly mad about her face, Martha decided. Something unhinged. Her eyes weren't the eyes of a six year old, any more than the eyes of the boy had belonged to a nine year old; but the boy had been godlike (she could think of no better word for him), while this girl seemed tied together with rags. The black of her eyes was the only coherent part of her.

"You died here," the girl said.

"No I didn't," said Martha. She hesitated. "I didn't."

"I can see what you are."

"I didn't die," said Martha.

Was this true, she wondered? What else could parting company with your body possibly mean?

The girl smirked.

"Where's your angel?"

This filled Martha with confusion, not least because the girl had asked it so tauntingly.

"What angel?" she said. "I don't know! What angel?"

"*What angel?*" parroted the girl. "Why don't you know?"

"There was a boy," said Martha. "He helped

me. But he never said anything about angels."

"Tell me about him."

"A child, like you. No. Not very like you. A Being of Air."

"Well, *I'm* a Being of Air. *You're* a Being of Air, with no body and no angel. There are countless kinds of Beings of Air."

"What kind are you?"

But the girl chose not to answer this question.

"I bet he was jealous," she said. "Some of us are. The brightest ones. The proudest ones. That was mean of him, not to talk about angels."

"Mean?" said Martha.

The girl had now come much closer. Too close. Her face swam in Martha's vision. Martha was amazed to see what looked like dust on the girl's cheeks, and what must surely be the dried path of a tear running through it.

"We can lie, you know," the girl said. "And we can be spiteful. I bet this boy of yours didn't tell you *that.* What *did* he tell you? Did he tell you what's going to happen to you?"

"He told me I had to choose," said Martha. "I could go back. My body's in a hospital."

"Or?" the girl said.

"Or I could drift. But I won't drift. I came here, all on my own. I moved through Air. He was wrong about that."

The girl shrugged.

"It pulled you. The place where you died

pulled you. Other places will do the same. And when the pull fades away, the wind will take you."

"No," said Martha. "I decided to be here. I willed it."

But now, she was starting to doubt herself.

"And what was the third choice?" said the girl. "I bet there was a third choice."

"To go on. To go up."

The girl was smirking again.

"Well, for *that,* you'd need your angel. But it looks like your angel's gone, little girl. It's abandoned you. If the boy gave you choices, he was lying. If choices were ever available to you, the time you could make them in has run out."

With a lip-curl of self-satisfaction, the girl moved away. She appeared to sit down on the bridge's metal shelf, in exactly the spot where Mark had sat, and started combing through the tangles in her hair with the thin spikes of her fingers.

Martha shook with indignation. What was she to believe? Was the world so ordered – so universally mismanaged – that even here, wherever *here* was, in the realm beyond living, she still had to struggle with confusion, with sorting truth from lies?

"Take me to my angel," she said.

The girl regarded her doubtfully. Martha repeated it.

"Take me to my angel."

"It's gone," the girl said.

"Gone where?"

"Wherever angels go. Out of Air. Up."

"So take me."

"I can't."

"Take me!"

The girl left the shelf and floated back towards her.

"We're in Air," she said, with a tight little grin. "We're *of* Air. We can't go further."

Martha thought for a moment.

"You said you could see what I am," she told the girl. "Well, what am I? Tell me what you see!"

It was the question she'd asked the boy, but the answer she got now was quite different. The girl threw her head back and laughed.

"I see practically nothing," she said.

She poked one finger at Martha, and the finger went right through her.

"No," said Martha.

She moved.

It was easier the second time. All it took was determination; and as she moved, Martha found herself wondering if she'd ever done anything with real determination during her life inside her body, or if it had all just been drifting. Not even jumping had been determined, she thought. Not really.

The girl was now below her. Suicide Bridge

was below her, getting smaller and smaller with incredible speed. The gorge became a single rip in Earth. The cycle track stretched to a long, thin line and vanished.

Clouds thronged about her, for a moment.

Then she was somewhere else.

13

When Martha was about five or six years old, Mark read her *Alice in Wonderland* by Lewis Carroll. Her brother and her mum used to take it in turns to read to her when Lionel was working nights. Martha fell in love with *Alice,* although a lot of it must have gone way over her head. Just the sheer strangeness of it held her spellbound.

When Joan said her goodbye, there on the beach in Whitstable, it felt like Martha was watching the White Rabbit scuttling away down his hole. The White Rabbit: a nervous, twitchy thing, not all that much like Martha's mother really, but maybe you can see that she imagined they had the same kind of liveliness, the same kind of desire for *What's next?* So when Martha saw Joan make that goodbye, she chased her. *Come on,* she was pleading – not in words, she was only eight, but she pleaded daily in a hundred different ways – *Come on, mum, I know you've got more than enough life and love and zip for what's happening to us, please don't disappear!* But Joan didn't hear her, and Martha felt she was just watching her fluffy white tail going away into the distance. She'd turned to face something Martha didn't understand, and her fluffy white tail was all that was left of her.

She stopped going out. Mostly it had been her going out with Lionel, to bike races, or meeting mutual friends down the pub, but if she had any of her own friends, she must have started abandoning them, too.

Martha doesn't know exactly when the pills started, and she still doesn't know exactly what Joan took. Probably a cocktail. She drank, as well – not wild amounts – but there was always a bottle of white wine open in the fridge, and Martha doesn't imagine whatever pills she was taking would have mixed well with booze.

The result of no friends and a diet of pharmaceuticals was that Joan started fading. Martha was too distraught herself to notice at first. With the absence of Lionel, the whole world seemed changed in a terrible way, and if Joan was dead quiet at the dinner table and kept forgetting to pack Martha's PE kit, that was just a tiny part of how everything was suddenly awful. But Martha remembers when she first saw things for how they now really were.

She'd gone to bed feeling poorly. She was probably nine and a half by then. There was an itch in her armpits and a churning in her tummy, and a feeling of dread that no bedtime story could magic away. Her mum had read to her, and kissed her goodnight, and left. Then she'd lain awake for ages; then slept; then woken abruptly, and vomited. There was sick in her throat, in her hair, in her eyelashes: coating her pillow, drenching her pyjamas. She stumbled downstairs, still half asleep, and wailing.

Joan was on the sofa. She wasn't doing anything. No phone; no TV. She was just sitting, and she looked up at Martha very slowly, as if the muscles in her neck needed oiling. Then she just gazed at her. *Stared* is too strong a word.

Mark cleaned her up, and changed her sheets, and put her back to bed. He probably phoned her school in the morning, too.

Of course, Joan's first husband died tragically when Mark was still practically a baby, and her zip must have stayed, somehow, to raise him as she did – and to still be the person that Martha's wonderful dad fell for, six years later. Perhaps she'd put her misery on hold, somehow. Perhaps she'd used all her strength and spirit to lock it away, like stuffing a suitcase and having to sit on it to close the straps, until her second husband's own indefinitely extended holiday made it all tumble out again.

Martha doesn't know. She doesn't feel she'll ever understand her mum, not really, however much she loves her.

But she certainly ended up following her down that rabbit hole.

14

Somewhere else.

Martha felt like she was up in the higher reaches of Air again. Gales buffeted her. The sky – it wasn't really the sky, it was everywhere – was a twilight blue with luminous streaks of curling, flickering purple. It was breath-taking. It was gorgeous. And it was terrifying.

It wasn't just the silently howling winds and the strangeness that made Martha afraid. (The winds made no sound; or if they did, it was the sound made by a bomb blast, with your ears deafened and ringing.) Here, Martha felt *thinner*. She felt – she was *made* to feel – that there was something of her missing, and without it she was in grave danger of simply being swept away. Here, the boy's prophecy of her being shredded by the winds of Air until nothing was left of her felt like an imminent reality.

Again, the cacophony, the choir, of voices. Which were the winds' silent voices, too.

Look! A flame.
A flower.

What does it want?
How steady the flame is!

Martha didn't feel steady in the slightest, she felt on the verge of being snuffed out. But she took heart from this, and repeated what she'd said to the girl by the bridge. She could barely hear the sound of herself, but she knew she was heard.

"Take me to my angel!"

The voices seemed to draw back at this; seemed to converge into themselves, as if they were offended.

Martha spun, slowly: a single drop in a wide, wild ocean.

This is the one that was helped.
Not our problem.
One of us made it his problem.
She can't be helped.
One of us made it. Where is he?
Where is he?

But there was no answer to this question. It had sounded like a summons, a call, but still no answer came.

A long time passed, or seemed to pass; but then Martha saw that a shape was forming itself out of the strands of purple in the sky around her. These strands knotted themselves together, making a body, and then limbs, and a tail. The body was the stretched *s* of a snake; the limbs were clawed; the tail glittered and snapped like a flag. The head, formed last, was monstrous. It was over-sized, with cavernous eyes, and elongated fangs in a gaping mouth.

The shape was a dragon. Its head loomed towards her. When it spoke, its voice was like gravel churning on a wave-battered beach.

"You should not be here," it said. "You are breaking the rules."

"What rules?" she said. "The boy, and the girl, they both talked about rules. But neither of them bothered to explain them to me."

The dragon breathed a sigh. Martha flickered, and nearly went out.

"Look, I'm sorry," she said. "I'm sorry for all of it. I died. I shouldn't have died. I said no to what happened next, and it seems like that was wrong, too. I've said no to my body, and here I am now with nothing much left. But I'm trying my best. That's all I've ever done. And so I'm simply asking you: where is my angel?"

Martha knew that the creature before her possessed no flesh and blood. She knew that it was an illusion, made possibly by these Beings just to intimidate her. But now she understood too what the boy had tried to tell her, that the surface of things was also their reality, and that this dragon could swallow her, annihilate her, should it choose.

Martha didn't feel very brave, right then.

The dragon spoke.

"We know nothing of angels. They come. They go. They are not of our element. We are Beings of Air. We cannot help you."

"Then who can?" said Martha.

The dragon paused before it answered. The holes of its eyes seemed to turn in on themselves.

At last, it said:

"Go back to the boy. Go back to Earth. He will help you find a shape."

"A shape?"

"An appearance. A skin."

If Martha had had a head, she'd have shook it; but the Beings understood, nonetheless.

"Without a skin, you will certainly become nothing. Frankly, we're amazed that you can be here at all, as you are. Find a skin, human soul. Then, if you still desire it, you may return, and call for your angel."

With these words, Martha felt herself beginning to disintegrate. There was a hollow in her chest – but she had no chest – where the winds screamed through and away into unfathomable distances, pulling her with them from the inside out.

The dragon was right. She'd been presumptuous. She'd dared to be above herself.

She needed to move.

Away, thought Martha. *Down.*

And then:

The boy.

PART TWO

1

So this is a bonus chapter. An extra. Believe it or not, I've now finished this whole book, but something's been bugging me, as I've read back through what I've written. Although I've shown Mary almost all of it, she hasn't seen the very final chapter, and obviously, she hasn't read this one, either. She's also heard my story as I originally told it, there in the counselling room at the CAMHS unit. This book was made at her suggestion, and for her sole benefit; so you have to bear in mind – and *I* have to bear in mind – that when you see *Dear reader,* she's the person I was thinking of.

Only now, she's suggesting putting it out there, for anyone else who might want to look at it. This means I've had to re-imagine a few things

– just a few – and try to put myself in the place of a reader who never met Martha, doesn't know anything about her, and most importantly, never got the chance to listen to her voice speaking the first version of this story: the one that only exists now in Martha's and her counsellor's memories.

The result of all this re-thinking is that I've decided to go back and add these few words for the benefit of you, dear reader.

Just you.

Mary really struggled with this story, the first time. So to be honest, I'm wondering how you're coping!

I want to warn you that it doesn't get any easier. I want to warn you that things just keep on happening, one after the other, and that if there doesn't seem to be any rhyme or reason to them, any pattern, any plan, then that's because there wasn't one, or not one Martha could work out while she was in the middle of them. Perhaps it will help if you remember that Martha, of course, was in exactly the same position, struggling along through her own story – trying to write it for herself, but most of the time having it written for her – and just as mystified and frustrated and all at sea as I'm imagining you are.

Truth is stranger than fiction, supposedly. I could assert the truth of this story till I'm blue in the face, but I realise I can't count on you believing me. And yet maybe – although I ought to admit that it's taken me a long time to come to this conclusion, because you're going to hear about various arguments I had with Mary on the topic – maybe, believing or not believing doesn't matter. Not to me, at least, because I don't even know you. But perhaps, dear reader, not to you either.

A wise person once said (quite a few of them have said it, actually) that fictional stories are truer than factual ones. They tell us larger truths; truths that are true for everyone. So you might look at this way, and if you do, I've got no problem with it: the stories we find easiest to believe are the ones we believe are made up.

2

All that was left of Martha Mud found herself hovering above a city. It was a truly enormous city. She still can't guess which one it was. There was the broad sweep of a bay, and white tower blocks; there were criss-crossing thoroughfares, and traffic, and the atoms of pedestrians moving along pavements. Beyond the city's geometric centre, a jumble of flat-roofed slums spread out like ripples, on and on.

And there he was.

The boy was different. He looked quite a lot older, for one thing: there was a fuzz of moustache above his lip, and an emergent leanness to him, as if something were trying to push its way out of him. But somehow – Martha couldn't deny seeing it – he was smaller, too. Reduced. His limbs still shone, but the light in them pulsed, now bright, now dim, as if at the beck of a sluggishly beating heart. His face was downcast.

"You," he said.

It was an accusation.

Martha swam circles around him. She was

showing off, but she wishes now she hadn't.

"Look!" she said. "You were wrong. I can move."

"So I can see," said the boy.

"I moved, and met a girl. She told me about angels. Why didn't *you* tell me about angels?"

The boy just shrugged, and Martha had an urge to thump him.

"She also told me you can lie," she said.

The boy looked straight at her, and Martha was amazed to find his once glittering eyes were now flat and guarded.

"Of course we can lie," he said.

"Oh. So were you lying when you told me I was stuck? That I couldn't move without your help?"

"I told you what I knew. I explained the rules to you. But you broke the rules, and look what it's done to me. You've changed me."

Martha felt his bitterness like an icy little draught. What was going on? she thought. Yes, the boy was bewilderingly different, but why was he blaming her for it?

"I don't understand," she said. "Tell me. Talk to me." And when the boy didn't answer: "I wish I knew your name. I wish I had something to call you by."

"Yes, give me a name," muttered the boy. "Give me a name, and make your sabotage complete."

Martha couldn't think what to say. They

hung together above the buildings of the metropolis. Black smoke billowed from factories on its outskirts. Blue-grey hills ringed the far distance, sketchy and uncertain.

"Look!" said the boy suddenly. "Look how many of you! A million die in a moment, and a million born. Too many. A pestilence. Too many."

Again, Martha couldn't answer him. Perhaps he was right; but his words just made her think of her own family: how *few* there were of them. How lonely she'd been. Her mum. Her brother. Her absent dad.

The boy turned on her.

"A plague of you, and there's nothing to be done. Earth is sick of you. Air is tainted. If I were an angel, I'd fly as fast and far upwards as my wings could carry me, and never look back."

"What's happened to you?" she asked.

"You," said the boy.

"You have to explain," said Martha. "I don't know what you mean. I don't know what I'm supposed to have done."

"I shouldn't have let you see me," said the boy. "I shouldn't have tried to help you. It was nothing but vanity. You've thickened me. You've coarsened me."

Martha thought of the girl she'd met by Suicide Bridge. There had been something coarse about her, too. Something adulterated.

"I tried going back up," she said. "I nearly lost myself. I wish you'd been with me. The Beings there called to you, but you didn't come."

The boy looked devastated.

"I didn't hear them!"

"They told me to come back and find you," said Martha. "They told me you need to keep helping me. I'm sorry if being near me has done something bad to you. But *will* you help me? I've got no-one else to ask."

The boy grimaced.

"What," he said. "What did they say to you."

"They told me I need a shape. Something that will keep me from disappearing."

"To what end?" asked the boy. "You, a human soul, to remain forever in Air? Why would you want it?"

"No," said Martha. "It's to call my angel. I need to go as high as I can and call my angel."

"Your angel left."

"Yes! And I need to find out why! Tell me the truth. Why didn't you talk to me about angels?"

"I know nothing of angels."

"That's what the others said, but I don't believe you. Tell me what you do know. Tell me everything you *didn't* tell me."

The boy's lips twisted. It was a heartbreakingly ugly expression, on a face that when Martha had first seen it had been nothing but beautiful.

"This," said the boy. "And much good may it do you. Human souls ascend, or wander. If they ascend, they're taken by their angel. If they wander, they wander close to Earth, and their angel stays with them until both are swept away. But you are different. We found you near the place where Air becomes Water. As high as your angel had taken you, you refused to go higher, and your angel abandoned you. No angel abandons its soul. We could not understand it."

Martha, herself, was struggling to understand. She stayed silent, and waited for the boy to continue.

"I took you on. I made myself known to you. I acted your angel. So high you had travelled, yet then I discovered your body, in Earth, was still alive! I was dumbfounded. I stated your lawful choices, but in all honesty, I cannot imagine what choices were really open to you. O, human soul: your body will not take you back without your angel, and without your angel, neither can you rise!"

Martha groped for some thread of meaning in the boy's words.

"It never felt like a choice," she said. "It felt like a choice between impossibilities."

"It's all impossible," said the boy. "It's wrong and impossible from beginning to end."

"It is what it is," Martha said.

It is what it is. This was her mother's catchphrase. She'd used to say it about everything, from a grazed knee to the election results: at first, before Lionel left her, with a steely twinkle, as if things being what they were and not otherwise was something to be borne, for the present, and then to be fixed; and after, with a dulled resignation that used to seep into Martha's ears like cold porridge. She was surprised at herself for having said these words; and then, even more surprised to realise what she needed to say next.

"If I have to have a shape, I have to have a shape. How do I get one?"

The boy shrugged.

"In Earth, your body held your shape. Without it… I don't know. You'd have to make it."

"Make it, how?"

"By becoming. By being in Air. By doing."

Now he looked really hard at her. It wasn't easy, being looked at by the boy in such a fashion. It felt to Martha like she'd just stepped out of her back door into a winter gale.

"You've changed, too," he said. "You flicker. But you're clearer, and firmer." He shook his head ruefully, and the gale faltered. "You are nothing that I know. You can move! So keep moving. *Be* in Air. *Do* in Air. Perhaps you'll find the strength to gain a shape."

"Do what?" said Martha. "What should I do?"

"That's not for me to say. Doing comes from being. And I tell you again: I don't know what you are."

Once again, the sun was setting. Shadows from the city's tower blocks slanted over the sea. A million lights began to pop out of the darkness: a million embodied souls signalling to the night.

"Will you come with me?" asked Martha.

"Yes."

He said it mournfully.

"My name," she said. "You've never asked me my name."

"I have no use for it. But give it me, if you wish."

"It's Martha," said Martha. "Martha Mud."

"Thank you," said the boy.

He turned his gaze to the ocean, and Martha did too, but there seemed to be something still left unsaid. She looked at him sideways: this unwilling assistant; this substitute angel; this stranger. If Martha was a mystery to the boy, then the boy remained far more of a mystery to Martha.

"I meant it when I told you I wish I had a name for you," she said.

"Names are for things both higher and lower than me," replied the boy. "If you know something's name, you can call it. Names have been found, or given, to Beings of Air before. It's never ended well."

"It would help me," she said. "It would make it easier for me."

The boy seemed to be locked in a struggle with himself. Just for a split second, his face looked miserably ancient: the face of an old, old man whose life had been wasted.

"Can they want it of me?" he asked.

Who? wondered Martha. But, "*I* want it," was what she said.

"Then make me a name."

Martha was startled to find the boy's name already on the tip of her tongue.

"I call you Simon," she said.

3

Mary sits back in her chair and regards me quizzically, almost confrontationally, from behind her glasses. It's not an expression she's allowed herself to indulge in before, and I wonder why she's doing it.

"I'm not quite sure where this is going now, Martha," she says.

"It's going where it's going," I tell her.

The faintest trace of a frown tugs at the corners of her mouth. I can see that she wants to ask me again if what I'm unburdening myself of here in this little room is actually something I think really happened, or if it's a game I'm playing; a circumlocution; a way of talking about what I feel to be otherwise unvoiceable. Because this whole strange tale of my time in Air is a flash-forward for my counsellor. I still haven't talked about exactly what happened on Suicide Bridge in the minutes and moments before I jumped.

There's a good reason for this, of course. But Mary needs to hear the story through before she can appreciate it.

Except I can also see that my last declaration leaves itself wide open to the *She's just making it up as she goes along* hypothesis that I imagine Mary, as an experienced counsellor, has to stay open to. So I add:

"It's going on towards the end. That's what stories are supposed to do, isn't it?"

Mary's been awfully patient, so far, in regard to the big hole in my history I've left gaping for her. I've told her about my father and my mother. I've told her bits and pieces about my brother, which is all I felt I had of him anyway, until I met him on the bridge. All I had of any of my small family, if truth be told. But of course, the actual jumping is the buried heart of all these sessions. The actual jumping is the reason I'm here in the first place.

As soon as this book is finished, I'm going to give it to Mary to read. That was the point of writing it all down: for her to hear it again, but un-jumbled-up, and told in words that hopefully make more sense. Obviously, by the time she does read it, she'll already know how the story ends; but right now, she's still clueless.

"Okay," sighs Mary. "I can't deny that it's interesting. Although I have to say it's not always easy to follow. There's an awful lot of talking."

"I thought talking was what counsellors wanted," I say. "I thought talking was the whole point. What bits are you having trouble getting?"

"You were looking for a *shape?* Something to hold you together so you wouldn't be swept away?

And the boy told you...?"

"Simon said I had to *be* and *do* in Air. To hold my shape in Air, I had to become a bit like him."

"Okay. That makes a kind of sense. I think. And this business of names. Why did you call him Simon?"

"It seemed to fit," I say.

But that isn't good enough, for either of us. So I tell her:

"Simon was my dad's father's name. My granddad. I never met him."

Mary now has the grace to stay silent, and into this gap, more talking tumbles out.

"Lionel used to tell me bedtime stories. I mean, really *tell* them. He never read to me. My bedroom was stuffed with books – my mum was always buying books – but Lionel always said the difference between hearing a story told to you and just hearing a story read was like the difference between tickling a trout and trying to harpoon it. I don't know, he was Irish. Maybe it was in his blood. But he seemed to just have stories at his fingertips. Every night – when he was around – he told me something different. And he always began his stories with, 'This is one your Granda used to tell me...'"

Mary smiles, sadly.

"Just occasionally, my father used to make up stories for me. He read to me, too, mostly, but I remember the ones he made up best."

"Lionel might not have made up his stories –

I honestly don't know – but they were wonderful," I say. "He told them with so much passion. I loved every one of them. And there must have been hundreds!"

"So you named the boy after your grandfather?" asks Mary.

"Yes. Like I said, it seemed to fit. The boy was so fantastical that half the time it felt like he *was* a story. And the rest of the time, he was trying to tell me stories. About Air, and how things were. Although it felt like he wasn't ever quite telling them properly. I kept having to ask him to explain them."

"Well. I'm sorry if it feels like I'm doing the same thing. This isn't an easy story you're telling me, Martha."

"No," I say. "It's not. But don't worry. If you feel you have to hassle me for explanations, hassle away."

Not an easy story... And now, of course, I'm wondering if trying to write it all down was such a great idea. I should have seen this coming, shouldn't I, naming the boy as I did? If Lionel was right, then all my painstaking editing and ordering and choosing of words is only going to end up murdering this strange fish of a story.

But perhaps Mary will tell me that writing it down was for me, not her. Or perhaps Mary – being honest – will tell me that this story's less of a trout than a great white whale.

4

"Where are we going?"

Martha didn't answer him. Simon. The boy. The Being of Air. She didn't answer him, because she was afraid to articulate the enormous desire that was the answer to his question. And she was afraid to voice it, because she was terrified that voicing it might somehow make going there impossible.

To find my father.

These were the words Martha Mud thought, but didn't say.

Why did she want to find Lionel? Why was this desire she felt suddenly so imperative? Martha had no idea. Once upon a time, wanting to find her father had been all consuming, but then it had dwindled to nothing and vanished, just like almost every other desire she'd felt since Lionel left.

Now it had come back again; come back with a vengeance. Why didn't matter. She couldn't refuse it.

For a little while, she couldn't decide how to

go about doing it. When she'd moved in Air the
first time, her destination had arisen powerfully
and out of nowhere. Perhaps the girl had been
right: perhaps the bridge had simply drawn her
like a magnet. When she'd moved the second
time, Martha had felt a little more in control.
She remembered picturing the oddly coloured sky,
and imagining the wind, and thinking *Up,* and
somehow, it had worked. But now, she had no
idea exactly what to picture. "Kentucky" was just a
name in an Atlas, and there was no guarantee that
Lionel was still living there.

Perhaps, if she just imagined him clearly
enough…?

She called to mind his face, which was easy.
But how might eight years have changed it? She
found it was simply impossible to visualise that
face any differently to how she remembered it.
Grey hair, no hair, the puffiness of weight gain,
a beard even: they were all just notions, and
wouldn't attach themselves to any plausible stab at
reality.

A thought struck Martha, then: what if he
was dead?

The boy she'd named Simon seemed to be
getting impatient. A slightly comical scowl was
crinkling up his forehead.

Martha decided to hold tight to a memory.
It was one of her earliest memories. She couldn't
have been more than four years old. She'd been
walking with her father in a park, and she'd

climbed onto a low stone wall. This wall had risen in stages, and she'd kept skipping along it and kept stepping up, until at a certain point she'd realised how terrifyingly high she now was from the ground. She'd yelled, and her father had held out his long arms to her and grinned his wolfy grin.

Jump! he'd said.

And how trustingly she'd done it! She couldn't recall the tiniest flutter of hesitation. And of course, he'd caught her, and laughed, and spun her round and round.

So Martha hugged this memory close to her, and willed herself elsewhere. She felt Air move through her, and herself move through Air.

But it didn't turn out at all how she'd planned.

"Oh," said Martha.

Simon stared down at where they'd come to with an expression at once puzzled and slightly squeamish.

"A house," he said. "Why have you brought me to a house?"

"I didn't mean to," said Martha. Her disappointment was overwhelming. "It's my house."

It was her bedroom, just as she'd last seen it: silent, and still.

"This is where I came first of all," she said.

"Before I started falling upwards."

She glanced at the ceiling, which was just a hands-breadth away from her – they were floating above her bed – but the ceiling was no longer sky, it was the familiar artexed plaster whose bobbles and whorls had become an ineradicable part of every sleepless night and bored afternoon of Martha's brief life.

She looked down again, and her gaze was drawn to the photo on her bedside table. It was Lionel enthroned on his pride and joy, his motorbike, legs splayed wide and every tooth bared.

Was it this that she'd moved to? A photograph? When she'd wanted the living, breathing, cologne-smelling, wiry-armed reality of him?

"I'm sorry. This was a mistake," she said.

But despite himself, Simon seemed curious. He descended to the threadbare carpet until he appeared to be standing on it, and turned slowly with a keen, troubled stare.

"This is where you lived," he said.

"My bedroom. Yes. Since I was little. All my stuff's here."

"Walls," said Simon. "It's so... *hemmed in.*"

Martha couldn't help but agree with him. Simon jabbed his finger angrily, as if his gesture could push the walls of the small bedroom wide.

"Your builders knew what they were doing. They had a vision, and they turned it into fact.

This is Earth at its stubbornest. Closed in on itself. Denying the reality of anything else."

He drifted to the window and looked out at the street and houses opposite. He laughed.

"Rows and rows of them! So many!"

"It's a town," said Martha. "It's how we live."

"I know how you live. I spin clouds out of who you are. I know everything about you. But until I took you to your body, I'd never actually *descended*. I'd never been so *close* to it."

Simon's eyes were filling with something like dread.

"Walls," he said. "Walls of Earth. This is how it must feel like. Forgetting. Believing this is all there is."

If Martha had known then what would happen later, she would have paid more attention to Simon's anguish. She feels, now, that it was anguish. Anguish is a powerful word. It means choking: a constriction of your windpipe so that breathing becomes impossible. But Martha wasn't really thinking of anything except finding her father. This bedroom, this little relic of her life, held only his absence, and she wanted to leave it.

But then something else happened, which more than distracted both of them.

The ancient smear of brown that was the chocolate stain on her quilt grew eyes. After the shock of seeing them, Martha recognised those eyes. Then the stain began to wobble, as if it was under water, and a whole face appeared in it. The face was quickly followed by a body.

"You," Martha said.

Simon drew back, and for a moment, his skin became dazzling: just as it had been in the higher reaches of Air, when Martha had first met him.

The little girl who'd formed in the rumples of Martha's quilt grinned slyly.

"Hello," she said. "Sorry, but I followed you. I couldn't at first, you went too high, but when you came back down again it was easy. I knew you'd have to come back down again. Aren't you pleased to see me?"

The girl had floated out of the bed, and now she hung between Martha and Simon. In all her orphan desperation, she looked exactly the same as she'd looked by the bridge.

"No. I don't think I am pleased," said Martha. "Why are you here?"

The girl ignored her. Just as Simon had done, she stared round at the bedroom. But while Simon had been aghast at what he saw, the girl seemed to take it all in hungrily, and with delight.

"This was yours," she said. "It pulled you. I told you places would pull you."

She moved to Martha's wardrobe and slid through the crack between its doors. In a moment she was out again, her eyes dancing.

"Clothes!" she said. "So many shapes and colours! Such *making* you do. Such mastery of your element. Will you give me one of your dresses, human soul?"

The boy found his voice.

"Send it away!" he said.

"How can she?" sneered the girl. "She can't. No more can you. You've lost your authority, *Simon.* This human soul's named you."

The girl giggled.

Martha was at a loss. There was too much going on here that she didn't understand.

"What do you want?" she said.

"I want to be different," said the girl. She shrugged sadly. "Look at me. Who wouldn't? But what do *you* want, human soul?"

"Don't answer," said the boy.

"I'm trying to find a shape," said Martha.

"A *shape?* Out of the nothing you've become? Well, good luck. You'll need it."

"Look," said Martha, "I don't think you're welcome here. I don't think we can help each other. Why don't you just go?"

The boy wrung his hands. He seemed genuinely distressed by the girl's presence.

"We must go ourselves," he said. "We must go quickly. Let me take you…"

"No," Martha said.

The girl was now hovering by the bedside table. She drifted forwards, and pushed her face close to the photograph that rested there.

"Father…" she whispered.

"What are you doing?"

The girl's lips were so near to it, Martha almost expected her breath to mist the glass.

"You want to know where he is," the girl said. "You let him leave, and now you want him back. Just like your angel."

"Is that true?" asked Simon. "Is that why you came here?"

"Yes," Martha said.

The little girl floated away to the window, turning her back on them with a teasing smile.

"Do you want me to find him for you?" she said.

5

It was as if the boy had grabbed her by the hair and yanked her upwards. When he'd moved her in Air before, it had been as gentle as a breeze carries thistledown. This was a sudden, violent buffet that knocked her sideways. She felt uprooted.

They were several yards above her house. Martha could see tiles missing from the roof, and the spattered television aerial where the starlings gathered.

She rounded on him in a fury.

"Don't you *ever* do that to me again!"

"I'm sorry," said Simon. "You wouldn't listen to me. I told you we had to go. Now we must go further."

"Why?"

"That thing below us is dangerous. You're not safe, human soul. And neither am I."

"What thing? You mean the girl?"

"It's no more a girl than I am a boy!"

"Then what is it?"

"A Being, but a degenerate one. It's fallen, and it's hungry, for what I don't know. But if it followed you, it must want something from you."

"But she said – "

The boy interrupted.

"You mustn't listen to it! You mustn't talk to it! Everything it says will be lies! Now, *move,* or I will leave you!"

Martha looked at Simon with dismay. The girl, the Being, the thing in her bedroom had offered to take her to Lionel. What if she really could? Ever since she'd been told to *be* and *do,* to find a shape, seeing her father again was all Martha could think of. And yet the boy seemed to have real fear in his eyes. Fear, and urgency.

Reaching a decision she hoped she wouldn't regret, Martha saw a place in her mind's eye, and allowed herself to be there.

Everywhere is Anywhere.

Now she was high above a hill. Clouds all but obscured it, but Martha knew it was there. Slowly, she descended, until the clouds grew thin and the hill began to reveal itself.

Curling green treelines like water; the straighter edge of a road at the hill's base, and meandering paths flowing up around its sides. And there, directly beneath her, the footworn clearing at the hill's top, and the small circle of standing stones like a sigil, an imprint, stamped in the turf.

This was a place where they'd holidayed once, all four of them. Martha remembered the pub they'd stayed at, and the long rambles they'd pieced together from locals' advice and a dog-eared map. Lionel hadn't brought his bike, and perhaps it was just her imagination, but after a few days away from that snarling machine of his, he'd seemed to grow lighter and thinner and breezier. She had an image of his long legs ranging over heather; of him standing at a viewpoint and then suddenly spinning like a kid, his arms helicoptering in the clean country air.

They'd picnicked here, at this very spot, at the centre of the stones. Martha remembered the silence: just the wind in the trees, and the odd bird calling. And Lionel and Joan had been uncharacteristically silent too, but not in the same way they were silent after they'd been arguing. Even Mark had been smiling, and then he'd giggled when his overheated ginger beer fizzed up his nose. Martha had felt something on that day that she hadn't felt since. It had been an intense kind of clarity. A realisation – and how simple it was! – that *this* was a family, and that nothing – not words, or gifts, or even any obvious acts of kindness – nothing at all was needed beyond each of them being there.

Simon was beside her. He turned, scouring the Air around them, and with an expression that looked almost grouchy, like a teenager looking to see who'd just jostled him.

"It's gone," he said.

"No," said Martha. "You've got to explain. You said she was hungry. You said she wanted something from me. You said she was *fallen* – what does *that* mean?"

The boy sighed.

"Fallen. Every Being can fall. Angels and humans and everything between. That creature was once like me, or nearly – but she craved something that wasn't hers to want, and so she fell."

Martha wasn't sure if she understood. She'd heard of fallen angels. Wasn't Satan supposed to be a fallen angel? Hadn't he tried to replace God, and been punished for it? She thought about how the girl had seemed to her. There'd been a meanness to her, and a tricksiness, but also a devastated frailty that Martha found impossible not to feel a tiny bit sorry for. Was this what had happened to her, or been done to her, when she fell?

Martha tried to feel her way carefully with her next question.

"You told me that in Air, appearance was reality. You said – " she tried to remember the precise words he'd used – *"the surface of things and the essence of things.* You said they were the same. But you're also saying that she's not a little girl, and you're not a boy. Well, sorry, but that's exactly how you appear!"

"Yes. That's how you see us, and that's how

we are. We are Images, and nothing but True Images. There are no false images in Air, and nor could there be. Yet I am no human boy, and *that* was no human girl."

Martha must have looked bewildered.

"What is the surface of a human?" Simon continued. "Your bodies. But your bodies are *just* surface. You clothe yourselves in bodies, and hide away your essence. Your bodies are no more your essence than the plants and skins and chemicals you wear. We, however, are able to hide nothing. We are surface through and through. We have no souls."

More questions echoed inside Martha at these words, but she found herself unable to voice them.

What is *a soul?*

What is the shape of a soul?

What's the shape of my *soul, that I'm now supposed to be looking for?*

All she could do was repeat, a little dejectedly, words the boy had already used about her:

"I don't know what you are."

The boy grimaced.

"Do not mistake," he said. "We desire, and exult, and mourn, and despair. We fall, and suffer. We mislead and deceive. We both harm and heal, and our harm can be terrible. And yet, with no souls, we will remain forever in our element. Unlike you, we can never leave."

6

I can see that Mary's gobsmacked by Simon's metaphysics. Gobsmacked. My words have struck her round the mouth, and now her lips move to feel the bruise.

"That's…" is all she can manage. "I'm not sure…"

"I know," I say.

For a moment, I wonder if she's actually going to try to wrestle with it. She goes quiet, and I can see her desperately searching for an angle of attack. But what she ends up saying, is:

"Do you know, Martha, what interests me most about what you've just told me is to do with your father. You said you wanted to find him."

Poor Mary. Having attempted to fly, just oh-so-briefly, with a bump, we're safely back on the ground of everyday counselling.

"I'm curious," she continues. "Didn't you ever want to find him *before* you jumped from that bridge?"

"Yes," I say; and I tell her.

Mary's relief is palpable.

I keep on talking.

Nothing ever felt right after Lionel's departure. Nothing. Not one single thing. If I say that dad took a piece of me with him when he went – a really vital piece, like a lung or a liver that I couldn't replace, and that I couldn't ever stop being aware of its having been ripped out of me – then that probably sounds melodramatic, doesn't it?

But it still feels true.

I know I'm not the only girl whose father ever abandoned them. Or boy whose mother abandoned them. Or child whose parents died in a car crash. But it *feels* like I'm the only one.

My dad was my world.

In the months after that daytrip to Whitstable, I probably asked Joan daily if she'd had any news of him. These incessant questions never made her angry. I guess, looking back, that was one of the signs of her disappearing. But the answer was always No, even if the No was just a sad little shake of the head, or a sigh, or a silence. It looked like Lionel had really and truly disappeared.

Sometimes, at first anyway, it was easy enough to pretend he was just off working nights. After a while, though, such pretending was impossible. Every breakfast felt like the prisoner's last meal, and every teatime felt like a funeral. Curled up in my bed at night, I'd try to tell myself one of dad's stories. They'd all been so vivid, it was easy to remember them. When the prince had slain the ogre, when the beggar had tricked the witch, I'd cry myself dry, and into long, troubled dreams of him.

But that can't have lasted terribly long, can it? We get used to anything eventually, and a year for a nine year old's almost a lifetime. So three of them passed, somehow, and I think I was almost twelve when I went to my mum and sat her down and told her how much I still missed him. Then I asked if she'd never had an address we could write to. The name of a biking friend. Some trail we could follow, however cold it might have become.

Joan looked at me long and hard when I'd said all this. I remember her long, hard stare went on for a long, long time, and because it was so unlike her – unlike the changed, vapid, rarely-meet-your-eyes mum I'd come to accept as the new reality – I started to wonder if what I'd asked her was about to precipitate some unimaginable reaction in her: tears, rage, screams, I had no idea. But no. She stood up off the sofa and went upstairs without saying a word. When she came down again, she was holding a piece of paper. An obviously old, slightly yellowed and crumpled piece of paper.

"His brother," she said, and gave it to me.

Then she went into the kitchen and closed the door behind her.

I had no idea I had an uncle. I knew Lionel's parents had died when I was only little; I'd never met them, although I'd seen them both in my parents' wedding photos. No other members of his family had made the trip to England for that wedding, and if they existed, Lionel had never mentioned them.

I was ecstatic.

I wrote straight away – I don't remember what I wrote, I hope it wasn't too desperate or embarrassing – and long after I'd given up hoping, I got a reply.

Here it is: word for word, apart from the names. With Mary in the CAMHS unit, I had to dredge my memory for exactly what it said, but right now, as I type, I've got it in front of me. I imagine Mary can tell me if I missed anything important out, but there's not very much to miss.

The letter was impeccably handwritten, in ink, with beautifully curly letters. Nothing like dad's, then.

Dear Martha,

Thank you so much for writing to me. I'm sorry that you had to wait so long for this reply – I moved away from the address you sent it to some years ago, and it had to chase me half way across Ireland before it eventually found me.

You asked about your father – Lionel Mud, my brother. That makes you my niece, and I can't tell you how wonderful it is to hear I have one! It pains me to tell you that Lionel and I parted company many years ago, and we've had no contact since. I knew from my parents – your grandparents – that he was getting married, but I'm afraid to say I wasn't invited. Sometimes families drift apart, through no particular fault of anyone. I loved your father, and believe he loved me, but sometimes life has a tendency to throw up complications, doesn't it?

Can I ask how old you are, Martha? Perhaps twelve or so, but I'm only guessing. Perhaps you're a little younger?

I'm not really sure what else to say, because I'm afraid I can't help you find my brother. I'm truly sorry he's walked out of your life, as he walked out of mine. He's a fine man, Lionel, but he always wanted more than he had, and probably more than he had good cause to ask for.

I hope you find him.

I have a house here in Kerry, and you and your mother would be more than welcome to visit, if you fancy an Irish holiday. I met your mother once, in a pub in Reading. That was when I was still spending a bit of time in England professionally, off and on, and just before your dad and I fell out. I wonder if you could ask her if she remembers me?

But regardless, please write and tell me how your search is going. Again, I'm very pleased that you've taken the trouble to get in touch with me, after all this time.

Sincerely,

Your Uncle,

Liam

So, that was that. I never showed this letter to my mother. I didn't see the point. I never wrote back, either. I probably should have, because poor Liam had to deal with his niece zipping out of his life the moment she entered it. But I was only twelve – he'd guessed my age right, anyway – and I was consumed with a longing for Lionel, not his brother.

Except after I got that letter, somehow, the longing just fizzled out.

"That was that?" says Mary. She's echoing my words. She looks a bit perplexed.

"Yes," I say. "I gave up looking. I gave up wanting to look."

"Weren't you excited to discover you had this long lost relative?"

"No," I say.

Mary's eyes through her glasses crinkle with concern.

"I'm not sure I understand exactly how you were feeling, Martha."

"I wasn't feeling anything," I say. "I just gave up."

"And Liam didn't write again?"

"No."

"And you didn't try any other way to get in touch with your father?"

"No."

A silence descends. I can see her little finger go up to her neck and start scratching – it's one of the things she does when she's thinking – but then it goes down again, and Mary folds her hands in her lap, and looks at the clock on her desk.

"It's time, isn't it?" I say.

"I'm sorry, Martha. Yes. It's time."

I know I'm not my counsellor's only client. Sometimes I wonder about them. I wonder if she listens to them as carefully, as intently as she listens to me, and if she does, how on earth she finds the energy. But at that moment, I'm simply checking the time for myself on my watch, and trying to decide if I'm relieved or disappointed.

And now I feel I should apologise to Mary, for not being able to tell her what I've just decided I'm going to try and write down here. I couldn't tell her because it wasn't something I'd ever tried hard to think about, and there in her little room with the clock ticking and the sunlight sliding through the blinds and my kind, wise counsellor waiting patiently for a revelation, all I wanted to do was carry on with the story.

But I can see now that if I'm going to tell it properly, the story needs this just as much as it needs metaphysics.

Here's how our conversation could have gone. Allow me to imagine what I should have said, and what my counsellor might have said in reply. Dear reader, I hope you don't mind.

"That was that?" says Mary.

"Yes," I say. "I gave up wanting to look."

"Wasn't it exciting to discover you had an uncle?"

"No. It wasn't exciting. It was just the opposite. All those tales dad had told me, warriors and wizards and rainbows and everything else, but none of them about *him.* How could he never have told me he had a brother? My dad suddenly felt like a stranger."

"That's understandable," says Mary.

"And Liam telling me that my dad walking out on us hadn't been the first time! Walking out on people was what dad *did!*"

"Were you angry at your father, Martha?"

"No," I say. "I'm angry now. I wasn't angry then. Maybe I should have been. The truth is, I never really felt angry about anything, I only ever felt out of my depth. I wasn't angry at Lionel. I was never angry at my mother. I wasn't angry at my brother, when he told me what he told me and demanded I try and help him."

"So you copied your mum. You closed the door."

"Yes. I closed the door. On my anger. On wanting. On hoping or feeling much of anything."

"Thank you, Martha. I'm glad you could tell me that. Perhaps... Does it feel like that door is beginning to open?"

"No," I say. "The door started opening when I died. It's been wide open ever since."

And now can I go on with the story?

7

Martha doesn't know how long she stayed at the stone circle. Time felt different in Air, but she couldn't say exactly how. She watched the sun rise and set, but she understood that the rising and setting was happening somewhere else. Day and night had no real meaning where Martha now was, and if Air had its own rhythms and cycles, she never became aware of them.

Sometimes, the sun looked just at it used to look, a bright yellow disc. At other times, it seemed that the winds of Air obscured it, and then it would pulse with colours that Martha had no name for. Just occasionally, it looked like a face that watched her. This face had no eyes, or nose, or mouth, but it was still a face.

Once, at midnight, she saw the sun regarding her quite clearly through the thickness of the darkened globe below her, and understood for the first time that Earth was no more and no less real than Air.

At some point during her stay, Martha realised something else: that although she could see the things of Earth, however altered they sometimes appeared, she couldn't hear them. The sounds of Earth didn't travel into Air. There were certainly other kinds of sound in Air, because she'd heard Simon and the girl and those other Beings speaking. She was also aware of the sound of a continual wind blowing, sometimes soft, sometimes deafening; but this wind couldn't belong to the realm of the physical, because here, everything physical was silent. Birds. Traffic. The chattering of hikers, come up to see the stones. Martha watched their mouths opening and closing, but no sound came out of them.

This surprised and unsettled her. She couldn't understand why she hadn't spotted it before. She tried to think back to the other places near Earth that she'd moved to, or been taken to. Her bedroom, first of all, whose silence had unnerved her. The bridge and the ocean were quiet places anyway, just like the intensive care unit. Perhaps she'd just been too bewildered, or distracted, or self-involved to notice.

She watched a robin on a sprig of thorn empty out its heart, and felt the grief of not being able to hear it go right through her.

Once, an aeroplane really did go right through her. Martha had no idea it was coming. It was a small little two-seater, quiet as any glider, but she saw the smoky trail it left behind.

So time – however much there was of it – passed in silence. Her thoughts were silent.

Sometimes a day seemed to have gone by, and Martha couldn't remember having had any thoughts at all. Lacking any body to wear out, she never got tired. She went on, never sleeping, and cars passed on the road below her, and hikers and dog-walkers came and went, and stars appeared and faded.

There were no dawns, as she'd once experienced dawns. There were no dreams.

But there came a point when she knew she couldn't stay at that place any longer. She knew she had to make a decision.

She called the boy.

He came as his name went out from her. She didn't know how near or far he'd been from her, but he was with her in a moment.

"I want to talk to the girl again," she said. "How do I find her?"

Simon looked unsurprised.

"I can't protect you," he said. "You know you can die here. Really die. Become nothing, forever. Or become something worse."

"I need to understand her," Martha said. "What she is. What she wants. I was told to *do,* and this is what I choose."

Simon shook his head slowly, but whether in denial or incomprehension, Martha couldn't tell. His eyes hung heavy in his face, and Martha was reminded suddenly of Joan, at breakfast, tired to the marrow.

"You'll find her in the place you first saw her,"

Simon said. "She'll be waiting for you."

"Will you come with me?"

"Do you want me to?"

"Yes!"

"Then I'll come," he said.

8

Martha moved easily and instantly back to the bridge. It was as much her moving, she decided, as her staying still, and Air spinning kaleidoscopically around her centre, until its motion slowed and a destination revealed itself.

The bridge: early morning, the sun burning mists from the hills and swallows sailing above her. And the girl was there, just as Simon had said she would be. (How had he known?) She seemed to be standing in the middle of the cycle path, head bowed, staring at her toes.

"Hey," Martha said.

When the girl looked up, Martha was amazed to see her expression. Gone were the knowingness and the cruelty, just for a moment. She smiled at Martha like a real six year old human child might have smiled at seeing Santa Claus.

"You came back for me," she said. "I wanted you to, and you did."

She said this so wonderingly that Martha laughed.

"Yes. I came back."

"Why?" asked the girl.

"You said you could find my dad."

"Well? Do you want me to?"

"Yes," Martha said. "Find him. Take me to him."

But the girl looked suddenly suspicious.

"Where's Simon? Did he come with you?"

"I think so. He said he would."

Martha looked, but she couldn't see him. The girl looked too, with a rabbity crinkling of her nostrils.

"No. You're wrong. He isn't here."

She smirked a little, then.

"Did you know he was a prince?" she said.

"No. What do you mean, a prince?"

"A lord. A ruler. I didn't think you knew."

"A ruler?"

Yet again – and especially with this child, or Being, or thing before her – Martha felt thrown far out of her depth.

"Air is a realm. All the elements are realms. And realms need rulers. Simon was one of them."

"Was?" asked Martha.

"I mean, before he got entangled with you. Before you *named* him. That's why he hates you."

Martha knew that she'd changed the boy, somehow. He'd told her so himself, although she'd found it hard to believe at first, and hard, in her innocence, to feel bad about. But by whatever incalculable mechanism, he wasn't now the brilliant Being who had shown her the clouds.

He'd become something else. And if he blamed her for it, why shouldn't he despise her for it as well?

"I don't understand why he isn't here," said Martha numbly. "He promised."

"Anyone can break a promise," said the girl.

"A ruler... Those others were rulers. The ones who became a dragon. The ones who told me to find a shape."

"Probably."

"And you?" asked Martha. "Simon said you're fallen. Were you...?"

The girl spat. Even though Martha knew this wasn't an actual infant, the grown up vehemence of her action was shocking.

"I've fallen nowhere," snarled the girl. "How dare he say I'm fallen!"

"I'm sorry," said Martha. "I wasn't trying to offend you."

But Martha found herself watching the ball of saliva that had seemed to leave the girl's mouth. It was still hanging in the space between them. Then it began to fray in the wind, and every strand of it turned into a tiny black insect. Whining like mosquitoes, they winged themselves away.

"*He* offends me," said the girl. "I'm just one of a billion. I'm nothing. I'm the lowest of the low. But that's not how I started, and it's not how I'll end."

Martha took a moment to make sense of this.

"A billion?" she said. "There's that many of you?"

"That many?" said the girl. *"That many?"* She snorted. "Your language has no word for it. Rulers must have subjects, and we are legion. Think of your Ocean. Think how many creatures it's stuffed with, from plankton to Leviathan, and then multiply, because every drop of Air's a creature, too. Didn't you know? Air is *made* of us."

Now Martha remembered the Beings that had become a dragon, and how they'd also been the wind. *Air is made of us.* Was it possible?

"Then why can't I see them?" she said.

"Because they've got no reason to show themselves to you. You're just a human soul, cast adrift in Air. They couldn't care less."

Martha looked up and around at the wide sky, knowing that the limits she could see of it – here, at the borders of Air and Earth – were just an illusion, and that the reaches of Sky were immeasurably deeper. She shivered. All of it peopled. All of it *living.* She remembered what the boy had said: *There is nothing not living.*

The girl had turned her back to Martha and drifted a little distance away from her. She seemed to be muttering to herself. Martha was beginning to feel deeply unsettled in the presence of this creature. Had she made the right decision in coming here to find her? And then she wondered: If the girl wasn't lying, then why had *she* wanted to show herself, when all those countless others hadn't?

When the girl turned to face Martha again,

her expression was nakedly calculating.

"If you want me to find your father, first I need a name."

"Lionel," said Martha.

The girl squinted at her, then burst out laughing.

"No! *I* need a name! *You* must give me one!"

"Why?"

"Because without one, I can't look. It's as simple as that."

Martha had given the boy a name. He hadn't appeared to want it, and having it seemed to have accelerated the sad and mysterious change that she'd watched come over him. And this girl, who now claimed she wanted a name of her own, had taunted him for accepting it.

But Simon had said she was hungry; that she desired something from her. Could this be what he'd meant?

"I don't understand," she said.

"You don't understand anything, little girl. Nothing of where you are. Nothing of *what* you are. I could try and explain, but you wouldn't understand that, either. If you want your father, give me a name. Then I can look. It's a straightforward offer. Take it or leave it."

Once again, Martha was left completely bewildered. She felt lost and alone and terrified, like a toddler she'd once seen adrift outside a supermarket, its face a mess of tears.

Where was Simon to advise her? What

should she do? What might happen if she made the wrong choice?

The girl came close.

"Give me a name."

"Veronica," Martha said.

PART THREE

1

Veronica had once been Martha Mud's friend. Ronnie was what her parents called her. Later, she became Nika.

Friend.

Well, dear reader. Maybe you can be a better judge of that than I am.

Martha had known her since they were both four or five. There was some connection between their parents to do with Lionel's racing, Martha never knew what exactly, but when her mum and Veronica's mum saw each other outside the school gates, they recognised each other, and that was the start of a string of play dates that went on until Lionel left.

Memories: playing princesses in Ronnie's

back garden. They'd raided Ronnie's dressing-up box, and then rushed out into the sun to chase princes and fight monsters, and to litter the grass with their bracelets and tiaras. They'd both just seen *Tangled,* the Disney film about Rapunzel and the tower, and they'd piled up crates next to the trampoline and found a long, blonde, candy-crusted wig. But which one of them was going to wear it? Which of them was the heroine?

They argued, but Ronnie claimed rights of ownership: her wig, her jewellery, her garden: her everything. Somehow, during the course of this bickering, Martha had managed to scramble right on top of the tower of boxes, and with the wig in her hands, she'd tried to argue the perfectly equal and obvious right of *I got here first.* Then, Ronnie pushed her. Martha can still see the flash of pure malice on her face as she stretched out her hands. The tower collapsed, and Martha just lay there in the middle of the wreckage, scratched and winded and too astonished to bawl.

Primary School. Martha was in Year 5. Their teacher was a grey-haired, wistfully smiling woman from New Zealand. She kept a little china kiwi on her desk, and her accent was gorgeous. Martha never once remembers her raising that gently rolling voice, and how she managed to hold a class of riotous ten year olds so effortlessly, Martha has no idea. Martha was in love with her. There was a day when everyone was supposed to bring in something for the nature table, and

Martha had found a bird's egg in a nearby park: a tiny, perfect thing of otherworldly blue, uncracked, but quite cold. She'd wrapped it in toilet roll and pushed it into her coat pocket, and had come to school with a fire of anticipation inside her.

But when her teacher called for contributions, she'd gone to her coat hook, and the egg wasn't there. Veronica had stolen it. There she was, at the teacher's desk, with a smirk on her face and that scoop of miraculous sky in her palm, and the teacher was delighted. Martha remembers the ensuing fight getting very ugly. Veronica wouldn't back down, and hair had been pulled, and hot tears wasted. Their teacher had lost patience with both of them. What became of the egg, Martha doesn't remember.

Thirteen years old. Martha and no-longer-Ronnie had followed each other to the same secondary school, although they were now in different classes. Still, at every break time they seemed to wind up together, with or without small groups of other girls around them. There was a boy in Year 10. He was drooled over by everyone. Martha and Nika had had many discussions about him, some of them giggling, some in hopeless earnest. This boy, of course, had never noticed either of them.

Valentine's Day, and Martha first became aware of odd grins from her classmates, and boys she didn't know pointing at her in the playground.

Then the boy's sister, in Year 9, had walked up to her and mocked her.

Mock. I've looked it up, and my dictionary tells me it means ridicule by imitation. Well, that's exactly what this girl did: she wept, and pined, and wrung her hands, and then nearly fell over laughing.

Why?

Nika had sent this boy a Valentine's card, and signed it with, *Undying Love from Martha Mud.* Martha just couldn't believe it. It was so petty, and so meaninglessly mean, and at the same time, so utterly ridiculous. It was so much like something that only actually happened in dodgy American TV shows.

And, of course, it was an all-out *coup de grace.* Martha had had to live with the fallout for months. She still can't think of that boy's face without feeling her cheeks start stinging with humiliation.

Well. These are three stand-out memories – grudges Martha could never manage to shake off – but maybe, who knows, Veronica could have come up with similar stories of spite and unfairness. Maybe, in Nika's world, Martha gave as good as she got. And telling just these three memories doesn't give the tiniest flavour of the long stretches of fun they had together, in between the fighting. It doesn't explain how close they were. Veronica was an only child, and so was Martha, really: both before Lionel left, when Mark had felt more like an occasionally indulgent uncle, and after, when he became something more like a replacement dad. So Nika and Martha dropped neatly into the twin holes left in each of their lives, and learned to bicker and connive together and push each other's buttons in a way that Martha imagines only sisters can.

Except, with Veronica, there was always something more. Martha still can't put her finger on it. A jealousy. An edge. Something dark, and secret, and bad.

Veronica moved away with her mum and dad some months before Martha died. The break was sudden and complete. They didn't even try to stay in contact.

Martha misses her. She misses her constantly, and at the same time, she's incredibly glad that she's gone.

But really, who needs friends like that?

2

There above the bridge, the girl ate her name. Martha can think of no other way of describing it. Martha spoke it, and then like a snake dislocates its jaws to swallow a rat, the girl gulped, and Martha watched as the twitching lump of it seemed to slide down the length of her thin little body until it finally stopped struggling. It took a minute or more. After it was done, Martha could see the name quite clearly, sat like a rock in the depths of her gut.

Veronica smiled.

"Thank you," she said. "Thank you, Martha Mud."

Martha stared at her, wondering what she'd done. The girl seemed no different, apart from the undigested weight at the core of her; and her eyes, which were now turned inward contemplatively, like a cow chewing the cud.

"Where's my dad," she said.

Whatever the true nature of the bargain she'd struck, Martha needed to make sure the girl delivered what she'd promised. *Take the money and run,* she thought. *Take the money and run.*

"Soon," said Veronica, because now it definitely was Veronica.

"How soon?" Martha said. "I don't know why you wanted a name, but I've given you one. You said you couldn't find my dad without it, and now you've got it. So find him."

Veronica's gaze opened outward, and she considered Martha for a long moment. Martha was reminded of the snake again.

"You'd have to let me carry you. I'd have to get close," she said.

"No," said Martha.

She was thinking of how violently Simon had jerked her up through her bedroom ceiling. What would it feel like to be carried by Veronica?

The girl was sliding nearer and nearer. She was closer now than she'd ever been.

"Don't worry, I'll be gentle," she said. "Not like Simon. I can see where he grabbed you. Just here. A sore place."

Suddenly, the girl was enormous. The bridge, the hills, the sky had all disappeared, and Air was nothing but the neckline of the little girl's dress, and the blue-veined skin that showed by her collar bone.

Veronica's voice rocked her.

"Oh, but you're so tiny! So nearly nothing! Petal. Ash-flake. How I'd love to wrap myself right round you. But I think I'd probably squash you, so maybe I won't!"

Martha couldn't breathe. She was about to suffocate.

"*He* hates you, Martha. You know that, don't you? But I think you're wonderful. Truly. You've just got to trust me not to hurt you, and then I can carry you wherever you want."

A reflex of pure terror pulled Martha out and away. The world came back again. Rapidly, she ascended, until she was hanging some way above the bridge.

Veronica raised her eyes to her with a small, crooked smile.

"I'm sorry," she said. "But I mean it. I love you, Martha Mud. You gave me something precious."

"I don't know whether I should have," Martha said.

Veronica shrugged.

"Now it's in me, I can hardly return it."

Much more slowly now, but with the insistence of a cat who's scented something meaty, the girl was floating back towards her.

"Believe it or not, that's the first gift I've ever received from anyone. Just imagine! Just imagine never knowing the love of being gifted with anything! Poor me! Poor Veronica!"

"Where's Simon?" Martha asked suddenly. "Do you know? Do you know why he didn't follow me when he said he would?"

"I have absolutely no idea," said the girl.

Veronica stayed just out of reach, and Martha

twisted with indecision. What should she do? Simon had been more than clear about not trusting her. He'd told her not to even speak to her, and now look what a strange web of words she'd got tangled in. But Simon had failed her, and for better or worse, this was what she'd chosen.

"Come here," said Martha. "Come closer. Not too close. Show me how you'll do it."

Veronica did as she was told. With an intent, unsmiling face, she reached out both her small hands, and as if cupping a moth, she folded Martha up and took her with her.

3

"Dark and secret and bad?" says Mary.

I should have known this would grab her interest. I shrug, noncommittally.

"I don't know," I say. "Those probably aren't the right words. I don't even know what I meant when I said them."

I think I've got Mary more or less hooked on this story by now. She's still got no idea where it's going, but it feels like she's become willing to suspend her disbelief; it feels like she's become more or less willing to believe that *I* believe. And because she's listening, I'm starting to enjoy telling it, however hard telling it keeps on being. So when she breaks the flow and asks me questions like this, I react, and come out with something obtuse. But I suppose she's doing exactly the right thing, really, from a counselling perspective.

So I say:

"I'm sorry. Those *are* the right words. At least, they're the best words I can come up with."

Mary now looks at me very directly.

"Was there anything sexual in your

relationship with Veronica?" she says.

Was there anything sexual? How could there not be? We were like sisters, but not. We were the same age, we hit puberty together (like a car crash), we spent all our time together. I remember sleepovers, pre-puberty, when we'd get naked once the lights were out and pretend-play being grown-ups, but we'd just end up giggling or bickering, there was nothing to write home about. When we started becoming attracted to boys – I mean *really* attracted – it was something that we shared, and often in intimate detail; but it was a passion for something else, something outside the pair of us, and it never spilled over.

I tell Mary all this, but she doesn't seem convinced.

"I'm struggling to understand," she says. "As usual."

She grins goofily at me: poor, dim-witted counsellor. Then she takes off her glasses, and starts to wipe them. This is another indication that she's trying to think. I'm beginning to love her for it, these little signs of her taking her job so seriously.

"You said that you gave the boy a name, and that you chose the name of your grandfather. Because he told you stories."

"Yes," I say. "And because Simon told cloud stories. He told the stories of people in clouds. I think I forgot to mention that was one of the reasons."

"Okay," says Mary. She smiles. "Yes. I get that. But why did you choose Veronica? I mean for the Veronica in your story? She doesn't seem... *nice.* Maybe she changes. But were you scared of her?"

"Yes," I say.

"Were you scared of your friend, Veronica? The Veronica who pushed you off that pile of boxes?"

"No," I say.

Something bad, and dark, and secret.

I pushed her lots too, and bit her and punched her, and stole things from her sometimes. She cried when I confronted her about the Valentine's Day card: really broke down completely, and begged me to forgive her, said she didn't know what she was thinking, said she hadn't imagined the trouble it would cause. (As if!) And then, next Valentine's, I thieved my first kiss from the boy she'd just started dating.

No. I wasn't scared of *my* Veronica.

Maybe the bad, dark stuff was only what we found reflected in each other.

And also, I can't seem to shake off the crazy feeling that Air Veronica was somehow the original; that she wasn't named for my friend, it was the other way around.

4

Veronica left Martha above another ocean. Waves heaved beachwards, where a small village clambered down to the shoreline from low green hills.

Martha looked for Veronica, but Veronica had gone.

It had been deeply unsettling, being carried by her. Although it was done in an instant, Martha had felt less like a moth being held in a little girl's hands than a midge tossed around by a hurricane. She'd felt *gripped*, and utterly helpless. This waif, this tear-stained child, was ferociously powerful.

But she'd gone, and Martha was alone again. She was happy to be alone again. She drifted towards the combers, dodging seagulls, peering at the houses ahead of her.

Where was Lionel?

This definitely wasn't Kentucky. It felt more like England: dull, damp, *weathery.*

She found herself drawn towards a single house just yards from the beach. It was one of half a dozen small, whitewashed cottages dotted along the shore, its roof tiled with mossy slate, its front door painted a bright, cheerful red.

Was this where he now lived? Looking at the house caused a fugitive kind of warmth to twist inside her. It seemed to be calling to her.

Martha tried to *see through* it: to look at it through the windowpane of Air, just as she'd looked at the sun when she was at the stone circle, and watched it put on and off its different disguises. But the house remained simply a house, and the waves on the beach below it rolled out, rolled in.

She was over its roof now. Its chimney was smokeless. A crow pecked among the slates, then took off and flapped away along the shore.

Martha's nerve was failing her. And waiting there for the courage to descend, her thoughts began to consume themselves.

What if this house wasn't her father's? What if she just dropped through the roof, unannounced (she could hardly ring the doorbell!), and found total strangers living there? Veronica might have brought her anywhere. She might have twisted the bargain to suit her own ends, and delivered Martha to a place that Lionel had once been at but wasn't any longer; or even (the possibility wasn't one she could ignore) the place where Lionel had breathed his last.

And *how,* in any case, had Veronica known to come here, when Lionel's own daughter did not?

But then Martha considered what would

happen if Lionel *was* living here; if below her, right at this moment, he was making a cup of tea in the kitchen, or watching TV, or sleeping in his bed. A bodiless human soul would slide through the ceiling and stare at him. That's all. She wouldn't even be able to hear his voice. She could never make herself known to him, and he'd just carry on drinking his tea, or flicking through the channels, or silently snoring. He'd get on with his life. He'd never have even the faintest suspicion that his daughter had finally come looking for him.

Be and *do* in Air. But what had she been thinking? If Lionel was alive, then Lionel was in Earth. In Earth, there was no longer any chance of being for her, and however much she might want it, nothing whatever that could be done.

Had it just been curiosity, she wondered? Was she just pruriently trying to find out what had become of him? Eight years was time enough for almost anything. He might have other children; other daughters. And did she really want to become a lurker in his life, passively scanning the posts of his daily acts but never logging on?

Was she seeking an answer to why he'd left, and never visited or emailed or wrote or called? Yes. Martha could admit this to herself. Yes, she was. But watching him boil the kettle wouldn't give her an answer. And neither, she knew, would seeing him tuck up another daughter into an unfamiliar bed, and then tell this other daughter stories that Martha couldn't hear, before he grinned that grin, and kissed her, and turned out the light.

A single car rounded the headland, and she watched its slow progress towards the beachfront houses. It didn't stop. It drove past all of them, down the road between houses and sea. She kept watching as it continued into the distance, until it burrowed into the curve of the hills and was gone.

Martha found herself shaking with impotence. She couldn't bring herself to descend into this human dwelling. She was unprepared for the possibilities of it, and she couldn't bear the certainties. She wanted her father more than anything – she knew this now – but she wanted him as he'd been when she was a child, and that wasn't possible.

Lionel was gone; and the human being who'd unwrapped that scooter and leapt into his arms and treasured his letters was now doubly gone.

Quietly, insistently, this house still called to her. But in despair, Martha turned and flew out towards the waves.

5

Far over the water, she saw a figure waiting for her.

Simon.

The boy was no longer a boy. Wisps of facial hair straggled amongst spots, and all his bones had pushed themselves into angles. With a shock, Martha recognised an odd similarity to her brother, about the time their father had left.

With another shock – as she drew closer – she saw that Simon was regarding her with distaste.

"Where did you go?" she said. "Why didn't you come with me?"

She was angry: at his expression, at his broken promise; and yes, even angry at his apparent growing up.

"I was stopped," he said.

"Stopped? What stopped you?"

"A monster," said Simon.

"What?" Martha couldn't hold herself back from laughing. "A monster stopped you? My dog ate my homework." She was convulsed with laughter, and with rage.

The boy watched her coldly until the spasm

passed.

"Explain," she said. "I have no idea what you're trying to tell me."

"The Being who you see as a child has got hold of a monster. The monster confined me, through that Being's will. I was defenceless. I was caged. That is why I couldn't follow you."

"*She* stopped you?" said Martha.

Could this really be true?

"It isn't a she. It's a fallen Being of Air. A creature."

"It's definitely a she," Martha said. "I gave her a name."

Simon grew pale. Martha could see now that his own anger went far deeper than hers: unguessably deep. It seemed to drip from the pores in his skin as he stared at her, and sobered completely by this realisation, Martha waited for him to speak.

But what Simon said, was:

"Human soul, you have committed a great evil."

A great evil.

No.

"That isn't fair," she said. "I had no idea. And I only did it to find my father."

"So you lied to me," said Simon. "You told me you only wanted to study her. To understand her."

"I do! I did!"

Martha went quiet. He was right, she had lied. And having anything at all to do with

Veronica, let alone making a deal with her, had all been against this other Being's advice: Simon, the first to receive a name from her. Her guide. Her teacher. The one who'd elected to help her, and at what strange cost, she still couldn't guess.

And after the bargain was struck and the deed was done, had she got what she wanted? Had she found Lionel?

"I'm sorry," she said. "I honestly didn't know what I was doing. But I still don't understand. What will she do with a name?"

"There are many things she *could* do. I'm not sure what she desires, although I'm beginning to guess. A name gives her power. And just think what power she already possessed, to harness a monster!"

"But I gave you a name," said Martha. "And it looks like it's made you weaker."

"We are very different, that creature and I. The power of a name given by one such as you isn't lawful. I think she will choose to use it. I must choose otherwise."

"You mean, if you wanted…"

Martha looked at him, but the bleak reproach in his eyes was more than she could bear, and she looked away again.

"Tell me what you mean by *monster*," she said. "It seems I don't know anything."

"Monsters are what *you* make," he said quietly. "Human souls, in Earth. Monsters are the greeds and loathings and cruelties you pour into our element. They are not Beings. They are pollutions. But with the right kind of knowledge, and the will and the strength to do it, they can be tamed, and used."

Martha considered this. Air kept confounding her. Every time she thought she was beginning to understand it – finding the boy, learning to move, confronting the rulers – yes, even bargaining with Veronica – some new aspect of it surprised her, and pushed her back to square one.

"I'm sorry," she repeated. "This monster. What did it do to you?"

"Far less than *you* have done to me," said Simon.

Martha flinched.

"The monster humiliated me. As I said, I was caged. I was held until it was told to release me. Until my captivity had served its purpose."

"What purpose?"

"That seems clear. The giving of a name."

Oh. Of course. Simon would have stopped her doing it, or at least tried to. Martha didn't know what to say, realising glumly that all of her conversations with Simon reached this stage, sooner or later. Instead of speaking, instead of floundering for excuses, she tried to look at him: remembering what he had been, and what he now seemed to have become. His limbs were graceless, his expression both irascible and haunted. His skin had dulled to the same browny-grey as

Veronica's dress. He looked trapped by another kind of monster entirely: his own burgeoning body. However he struggled against it, it held him in a grip he couldn't escape.

Simon looked back at her. He appeared to be doing the same thing. Assessing her. Seeing through her.

"Do you know where she's gone?" he said.

"No. She left me here. She said she was taking me to my dad, but I wasn't even brave enough to find out if she was telling the truth."

"We should try to find her. We should try to stop the damage she intends."

"Okay," said Martha. "If it was my fault, then yes."

"We're alone," said Simon. "If I was as I once was, I'd climb up and enjoin all the Beings of Upper Air to help us. But we're entangled now, you and I. Martha. Martha Mud. I can no longer rise."

It was the first time Simon had called her by her own name. Martha felt herself shift, and glow: like hot breath on embers.

"I could go instead," she said. "I could go and ask."

"It's uncertain they'd listen. And I don't think you could do it safely, as you are."

Martha remembered how close she'd come to being taken by the wind; how nearly the dragon had consumed her.

"Then it's just us," she said.

"Yes," said Simon. "For now, just us."

6

When Martha was a very small child, her mother would hold her as if she was the dearest, perfectest, purest thing in the universe. Martha can still remember being held like that quite clearly. She thinks she can remember exactly what it felt like.

Her dad loved her – she truly believes this – but not enough to stop him leaving.

Her mum kept loving her, too, through all of it. But not enough.

Back when it was still the four of them, just occasionally, Martha and her mum would pull a sickie. That was when Joan still had her part-time secretarial job. Martha would have been five or six. On miserably rainy mornings, or on mornings when Joan maybe hadn't slept, or just for no good reason at all, Joan would phone in sick, and call Martha's school, and while Mark made his own breakfast and went off to catch the bus, she'd hollow out a nest of pillows and duvets on her and Lionel's bed, and curl the both of them into it, and together they'd watch films on Joan's laptop, while somewhere far, far away from them, the rest of the world went on with its business.

Martha doesn't remember the films. They were boring, talky, grown-up films, and she never really followed them. The films were far less immediate to her than the soft slither of her mum's night-dress, and her warm breath, and the yielding cushion of her breasts and stomach.

These were among the happiest moments of Martha's childhood.

Looking back, Martha thinks that they must have been days when Lionel had been away at work for a while, building his motorways. Joan needed comfort, needed not to be alone, and how wonderful that the comfort she needed was something Martha could give!

When Lionel left, Joan turned away from her daughter to other kinds of comforts. Jagged little consolations, Martha imagines them: prescriptions, and half a bottle of Chardonnay, and bed till late afternoon. But by then, of course, Martha was older. How was it that a nine year old, and a ten and eleven and twelve year old, was unable to supply Joan with what that five year old had given her?

Was it something Martha had lost?

Surely, if she'd lost something, wasn't it the duty of her mother to try to find it for her?

Martha, inevitably – once she was a little older still – found her own routes to the relief of being. She drank her mother's Chardonnay, knowing her mother was unlikely to notice it missing. She experienced, once or twice, the brief oblivion of sex. She discovered that there were other kinds of drugs than her mother's bottled tablets, and that these offered different and quite various possibilities of comfort, although she kept her head and steered clear of most of them.

But none of these avenues delivered the same feeling she'd had when she'd been wrapped up warm and tight in Joan's bedding. And inch by inch, Martha realised that the best and safest comfort could be found in *not* desiring comfort.

Not desiring comfort.

It wasn't as hard as it should have been; not nearly as hard as her peers and her mum and the whole world it felt like seemed to be telling her; and it got easier and easier the more she practised it.

What was practising it like?

That's simple to describe, because there's nothing *to* describe. It was simply being and doing nothing at all.

7

"How do we find her?" asked Martha. "How do we find Veronica?"

"Not easily," said Simon.

"Can't we call her? You told me if you know someone's name, you can call them. And I called *you*. At the stone circle."

"Because I assented to be called. Many of you humans have come to grief in that mistake, thinking that knowledge of a Being's name means you can command it. If we called her, Veronica would only come if she chose to. And if she chose to, she'd have reasons to come that we wouldn't understand until it was too late."

Martha tried to take this in.

"I can't find Veronica," said Simon. "But I think I can find her monster. If we're lucky, it will lead us to where she is."

Simon drew close to her.

"You must let me carry you. We have to go far," he said.

Not again! thought Martha.

When Martha Mud was in her last year at

Junior School, she'd gone to the leavers' disco. It was right at the end of the final term, and all the girls had been discussing what they were going to wear for weeks. Martha can't remember what she wore, in the end. It was held in some community hall; there were balloons and banners and fizzy drinks; what you'd expect.

The sound system was terrible, and the tweeny faux house music they played wasn't the kind of music Martha enjoyed listening to, let alone trying to move around to in front of her classmates. Lots of the girls were dancing, though, and some of the boys. Quite a few, like her, were standing around by the walls and the food table, watching.

At some point in the evening, she'd noticed that someone was standing next to her. It was Rowan Myers: a boy in her class who she'd only occasionally spoken to. He wasn't looking at her, but she knew without a doubt that he was intensely aware of her. He was standing much closer to her than he should have been. And then she felt him take her hand.

Believe it or not, it wasn't creepy. She let him do it, quite passively, and for a space of time – she can't tell how long – their touching palms made a warmth that spread itself right the way through her. It wasn't sexual, either. But it was nothing like holding hands with her mum or her dad.

Then she'd pulled her hand away, still not even having glanced at him, and went to find some crisps. If Rowan Myers was still around for the rest of the disco, Martha didn't notice him. On the last day of term, there was a moment when she thinks he tried to smile at her, but she'd looked away too quickly to be sure. He must have gone off to a different school after that, because she never saw or heard of him again.

It's funny what you remember; what you're never going to forget.

When Simon moved Martha this time, she thought at once of Rowan Myers, even though she didn't think she had for years. She didn't have hands, but whatever she was, was taken up and held. Shyly. Apologetically. And when the warmth came, as it did, this hold became mutual; because however such a thing might have been possible, Martha felt herself gripping back.

They were both of them high, high above range upon range of snow-covered mountains. It was night, and when Martha glanced up at the stars, they looked like silver fireworks.

"Here," Simon said.

At first, she couldn't see what he meant. Then a shape was covering everything beneath her. One moment it didn't appear to be there, and the next, it did. Because once upon a time Mark had tried to get her into Star Trek, Martha thought – a bit hysterically – of a Klingon warship decloaking. The shape wasn't there, and then, with a hint of a shimmer, it was; but as soon as Martha saw it, she knew it had never *not* been there. The mountains might as well have been a mirage, because this new thing she was looking at was much, much realer.

And now I suppose I need to describe it. Well, I've tried, and tried, but nothing seems good enough. It was vast: it oozed towards the horizon in every direction. Its swirling depths held vague, dismal lights. There were *things* rolling around on its surface like ghostly flotsam – eyes, and lips, and hands, and other body parts – that rose into view and then sank into black. It made no sound, but there was a heaving in the Air all around them: a laboured, lung cancer kind of breathing.

Martha, ridiculous as such an urge was for her, had a violent desire to throw up.

"That's the monster," she said.

There was no need for Simon to answer.

"It's…"

But Martha couldn't describe it, or explain it, or say how seeing it made her feel any better than I can. This thing shouldn't have been there – it shouldn't have been anywhere – but it was.

"Where's Veronica?" she said.

"I don't know," he said. "Not close."

"I want to go," she said. "I need to move."

"Wait," Simon said.

And just at the moment when Martha felt she couldn't endure being in the same place as this thing any longer, it vanished. Not like a Klingon spaceship. It had well and truly gone. It went without a trace, except for a muffled echo like an enormous, distant explosion. And there below her were the mountains of Earth again, their reality regained, muscular and honest.

Martha felt the essence of herself shiver and gulp.

"That's what held you," she said. "That was horrible. I didn't know..."

Her words dried up.

"She may have called it," Simon said. "We should pursue it."

"Yes," said Martha. "No. Not yet. Please, not yet."

Simon looked at her, half in pity, half with impatience.

"That's your creation. No-one else's. Not ours."

"Not *mine!*" yelped Martha.

"Perhaps," said Simon. "But it's a human thing, and you're a human soul. If we're to follow it, you'll have to be able to bear being close to it."

Martha thought about this. The shape, the monster, had been a worse thing than she had imagined could exist.

"I can try," she said. "But please: not yet."

8

"Hang on," says Mary. "I'm sorry, Martha. You'll have to slow down. I'm not sure I'm keeping up with you here."

I have to smile at this, because not keeping up was how Martha had felt too, and for pretty much her whole time in Air.

"This monster," says Mary. "You said it was man-made. Something to do with…"

"With all the shit we do, here in Earth," I say. "Yes. It was man-made."

Mary doesn't flinch at this word, but here in her counselling room, I'm sure she's heard far worse. Unless I'm provoked – and you'll hear more of this shortly – I honestly don't swear all that often. Sometimes I wonder if I'm the only teenager anywhere who doesn't. I'm not offended by it, but it just feels lazy, like using emojis so incessantly that they crowd out the English.

All the shit we do. Sometimes, of course, a swear word is exactly the right word to choose.

Now, though, Mary's looking at me with concern.

"Terrible things do happen in the world," she says. "Terrible things are *done.* But it's possible to dwell on them too deeply. To take them to heart. To feel responsible. And that can make you feel very powerless."

"Maybe," I say. "But that's not how I felt before I jumped. Before I jumped, I never even watched the news."

Mary takes off her glasses; puts them on again.

"Tell me more about the monster. You said it made you feel sick. Sick, and scared."

"Yes," I say. "Even if I'd been – I don't know – one of those people who obsess about Nazis, or paedophiles – I don't think it could have prepared me for it. Simon had warned me what it was. But not how devastating it would be, up close."

"And now?" Mary asks. "Do you still think about it? Do you have nightmares about it?"

"I don't have nightmares," I tell her. "I don't dream."

"You don't dream?"

"Not since I jumped. Not since my time in Air. No. I don't dream."

Mary corners her eyes a little at this, but decides, for now, to let it go.

"Do you wish you'd never seen it, Martha?"

"No," I say. "I'm glad I saw it. It was the truth."

"So do you watch the news now?"

"Only sometimes. Just enough to remind me.

It doesn't usually take much. But you don't really need the news, do you? Just walk down the street. Just open your eyes."

"Okay. So can I ask you about Simon? From what you've told me, he didn't seem to like people much. He didn't seem to have a very high opinion of humanity. Would you say you feel the same way?"

"Well, that's asking about me, isn't it. Not Simon."

Mary frowns.

"But I'll answer you anyway. The answer's no, I don't feel the same way. I think you're right. I think he hated us. But he wasn't human, and I am. How can I hate something I'm a part of?"

"Good question."

Once again, those glasses are off, and now Mary's rubbing her eyes. It looks like I've exhausted her. But I can see by her clock that my time isn't up yet, so I keep talking.

"Simon didn't stay hating us," I say. "By the end, I think he felt differently."

"Differently?"

"Simon was a cloud-creator. His whole purpose was to deal with the good stuff and bad stuff that humans send up into Air. He was ancient – I don't know, I never asked him, but there's no death from old age in Air, so I'm guessing he was immortal – and from his perspective, nothing ever seemed to get better. These monsters kept arriving, and each one was as bad as the last. They turned them into hurricanes. Air hurricanes, I mean. Hurricanes in Air. They blew them away. They cleansed them. But like he told me right at the beginning, it just never stopped.

"He knew his nature. He was proud of what he was. But he knew his nature was somehow less than mine. In the grand scheme of things, he was a servant, not a ruler. A Being of one element, nothing more. And having to deal with what he had to deal with, and knowing we were the cause of it... Of course he hated us. I would have as well."

"So what changed for him?" Mary asks.

"Everything, and for both of us," I tell her. "But to find out, you'll have to keep listening to my story."

9

They didn't wait long, there above the mountains. Simon wouldn't let them. What mountains they were, Martha never knew, but with the monster gone, they were beautiful, and she wanted to stay.

How, she wondered, could that tiny girl have taken control of something so enormous and so terrible? Imagining it was like imagining an amoeba trying to tame an elephant. But then Martha remembered how Veronica had hurled her through the void with such ruthless strength. Perhaps, it wasn't so inconceivable.

"Are you ready?" asked Simon.

She didn't try to question what she and Simon were doing. Whatever harm Veronica intended, Martha trusted that Simon would know what was to be done. Nor did she doubt that it was her responsibility to help him do it. Martha had encouraged Veronica, talked to her, struck a deal with her; the boy had endured that monster because of her.

Neither her trust in Simon nor her certainty that she should help him stopped her being frightened, though.

She took a deep breath – her essence took a breath – as Simon reached for her. She was trying to prepare herself.

They moved through Air together, still hugging Earth, and arrived above a town: buildings and parks and roads, with a motorway curving around its outskirts towards the smudged spread of a city in the distance. Martha looked, and felt a little tremor of dread. It was a view that seemed half familiar.

Yes: those hills behind them, spanned by a bridge. This was the town she grew up in. Martha was home again.

"She must be near," said Simon. "She must have brought it here."

"Brought it?" said Martha.

"Can't you see it?"

Martha couldn't. The Air below her was bright and empty; if the monster was there, the monster was invisible.

"I couldn't see it above the mountains, either," she said. "Not straight away."

Simon looked at her with distrust.

"How can you not see it? It covers Earth from edge to edge!"

Martha kept staring down, trying to sense its presence. Not being able to see it was almost worse.   Joan was down there, somewhere. Mark was down there. With an excruciating stab of guilt and fear, she realised suddenly that she hadn't really thought of either of them since she'd first arrived in Air. What were they doing, right now? Where were they?

"Why *here?*" she said. "What's she going to do with it?"

But Simon seemed to understand the panic in her voice.

"I don't know," he said. "But it can do nothing more in Earth. It's become a thing of Air, and it's to the Beings of Air that it's dangerous."

"All those humans down there. They have no idea. They can't see it. Nor can I! Why can't I see it?"

"I don't know that, either," said Simon.

"What happens if I go down? Go down, right now. Go through it."

"Don't," said Simon.

"No. I need to find my mum. I need to find my brother."

Martha was already moving. For just an instant, she felt Simon's hands catch at her, as if his fingers were tangled in her hair. Then his grip loosened, and she was falling free towards the buildings and roads and trees beneath her.

For another awful instant, she heard the roar of the monster's breathing, and felt a twisting wind inside her that might have pulled her into nothing, but somehow didn't.

Then the sound and the wind were gone. She was above the flat, white roof of a hospital. The silver stack of its incinerator drizzled grey smoke just beside her.

Martha took a moment to collect herself, then continued her fall, suddenly certain of who she would find.

10

But this next part of the story isn't any easier to tell than describing the monster. Martha's tried to find words for it twice, now. She told it once to her counsellor, stumbling and rambling, but Mary got distracted by everything Veronica said, and it felt like she was missing, or wasn't hearing, what was really important. Then Martha tried to write it down, in the spare, distant, this-happened-then-this-happened style in which she's tried to communicate so much of this story; but that seemed to fail just as badly, and Martha deleted it.

For most of this whole writing process, Martha's been assuming that the otherworldy, incredible parts of it are the hardest to put down truthfully; and they are, in a way. But in a very different way, the parts that are to do with her – just her – are far harder.

She's only just realised this. And it's something that her counsellor, being her counsellor, could probably have told her back on page one.

But she's going to try again. Wish her luck,

dear reader.

Lionel had been long and lean, and Joan was five foot four in her slipper-socks. Mark, though, was both broad and tall, with castle turret shoulders and thumbs like spanners. Mark was gigantic.

He'd always been bigger than Martha, of course – eight years' worth of bigger – but while Martha grew as fast as any girl can, Mark simply mushroomed, and couldn't seem to stop. It had been hard for him as a teenager, because his clothes always seemed to be just a little bit too small, and Mark had always cared about how he was presented. Martha remembers him groaning in front of mirrors, and badgering Joan for money to buy new outfits. He'd got used to finding his own clothes early, which was a good thing, because once Lionel left for Australia, Mark's unstoppable upward trajectory quickly outgrew Joan's capacity to shop.

By the time Mark was struggling with his GCSEs, he was taller than all his teachers. When he went off to college, he made his tutors look like schoolkids. Martha remembers that was the time when her brother started feeling responsible for her. He would knock on her bedroom door, and then – just fractionally – have to duck.

"Hey, little sis. Are you okay? How's your day been?"

These were always the words he used.

Martha loved that Mark was so enormous. He was like one of the friendly ogres in Lionel's stories; and when he read to her at night, the sense of this real-life, flesh and blood giant beside her often held her attention far better than whatever was in the book.

When he was nineteen, Mark got beaten up. A Friday night in town, and three kids cornered him after the pubs closed. At some point in the early hours, Martha was woken by a screech from Joan, and she'd crouched at the top of the stairs in her nightie while her brother dripped blood onto the carpet in the hall. His nose was squished, and one arm hung badly. Joan had just walked away, into the living room.

Mark was a gentle giant: the gentlest. Martha thinks that now, she understands why those idiots might have done it. She also thinks that probably, if he'd wanted, he could have given far better than he got. But she understood even then that although Mark had strength enough to topple towers, he didn't want to use it.

Martha adored her brother. He wasn't silver-tongued Lionel, and those bedtime stories should have been a disaster, when he was obviously as embarrassed by some of the silly books he was reading to his half-his-age, half-his-height half-sister as he was embarrassed by the fact that he was trying to take her father's place. But he stretched his length on her bed nearly every night, his feet lolling over the wood at its end, and made an attempt at comforting her. He made an attempt at trying to tell her they were still a family, and that things could still, for one evening, be alright.

Martha's brother made her feel safe. But when she dropped through the ceiling of the intensive care unit and saw him there, hunched on a tiny plastic chair at her body's bedside, she felt a hundred different things; but *safe* certainly wasn't one of them.

So what *were* the hundred different things? And it's right here that Martha's struggling to find the words for what she needs to say.

Surprise at not being surprised was the first of them. She hadn't expected to come back to this place, but as soon as she'd seen the hospital roof, she'd known that Mark would be here.

Why Mark, and not her mother? Martha didn't know; except that in the last split second of her descent, she'd heard someone calling. Not calling *her*. Calling *out,* like a bellow of pain.

Next, she was made to feel the strangeness of being so close to what was left in Earth of Martha Mud in a far more powerful way than when Simon had brought her here the first time. All she'd felt then was a kind of numbness. She'd acknowledged the reality of what she saw with a distant part of herself, but nothing else. This time, it was different. Her own brother was in this hospital ward, visiting her body; and almost as if she were looking through his eyes, Martha could now understand that it really was her body. She saw it in intimate detail: the bruise that obliterated the left side of its face, the tube pushed into its throat, the limp hair, the dulled skin. And even more, she now saw quite clearly that her body was *empty.*

All this would have been enough of a shock, but when she turned her attention to Mark, she saw, and felt, something else entirely.

Her brother had changed. He wasn't the same person who'd babysat her or bought her presents or helped her with her homework. Neither was he the same person who'd sent her that text, and tried to explain to her how unhappy he was. His great, hulking body was the same, but it was as if something bigger and stronger even than he was had taken a swing at him, and knocked something vital clean out of him. It was almost as if Mark's body was nearly as uninhabited as Martha's.

For a moment, Martha felt the whole world tilt sideways. Her brother was here, keeping watch over all that was left of his sister, and the experience was crucifying him. When Martha had talked to him on Suicide Bridge, she'd believed him to be helpless. He'd been angry, and lost, she saw now; but *this* was helpless.

Martha had been wrong. She'd been wrong

about everything.

11

There was another presence in that ward, besides the two nurses examining paperwork, and the three other human bodies that lay tethered to their own drips and feeding tubes and catheters: a presence in Air.

Of course, it was Veronica.

She was sitting on top of one of the machines by an empty bed, her back straight and her hands folded in her lap, and a look of wide-eyed fascination on her face. She was staring at Martha's body and at Mark, just as Martha had been a moment before.

Martha felt a crushing kind of dread when she saw Veronica. If Mark's presence here had been inevitable, then Veronica's presence, with all its assurance of bad things made worse, was surely inevitable, too. For a split second, like a match flame flaring and vanishing, Martha had a wild little urge just to flee.

Then Veronica looked up and met her gaze, and the instant was gone.

Martha flung herself down from the place by

the ceiling where she'd entered this room, every emotion she'd been made to feel since doing so now consumed by fury.

"Get out!" she hissed. "Fuck off, Veronica! Just fuck off!"

Veronica's lips curled, as if Martha was something sour she'd put in her mouth by mistake.

"Why should I?" she said.

"You don't belong here. You've got no right to be here. Just *go!*"

"No," said Veronica. "Fuck off yourself."

Martha turned helplessly away from her, back towards her brother. She was almost waiting for Mark to stand magnificently up from his chair and come striding over to sort this girl out for her. But Mark, of course, stayed where he was, hunched and oblivious: no more able to rescue Martha's body than he was able to rescue Martha.

"Sorry," said Veronica. "That was rude of me, wasn't it? But this is such an interesting place, and I don't want to leave yet. There's stuff I want to look at. There's stuff I want to find out."

"What?" said Martha.

"Well, I'm curious. To be honest, I've always been curious. What happens when Air and Earth meet? *How* do they meet? How do they get mixed up in each other?"

Martha chose to ignore this.

"Why did you bring that monster here?" she said.

"Monster? What monster?"

"Don't try lying to me, Veronica. I mean that sickening *mess* above us. Why did you bring it here?"

Veronica shrugged.

"And why did you make it trap Simon? Why did you trick me into giving you a name?"

Veronica narrowed her eyes at her.

"Look," she said. "I didn't trick you. We made a deal. Just the two of us. I didn't want Simon telling you all kinds of things that aren't necessarily true, so I stopped him coming. And as for the *monster,* it's just another part of everything that is, like souls and clouds and angels. Calling something a monster just because you don't like it is childish."

"It's disgusting," said Martha.

"No, it's useful. It's also conceived in Earth, but alive in Air. *That's* what I'm talking about. That's what I've come here to learn about."

This silenced Martha. She knew that the terrible shape above the hospital was made by humans – *monster* was the only thing to call it, no matter what Veronica said – and this knowledge made her feel ashamed. But she also remembered Simon's warnings about what this girl might want, and about what she might be capable of, now Martha had given her a name. So Martha said nothing, and tried, for the moment, just to *see* her.

The creature before her still looked like a very young human child, with a plain, tatty dress, and matchstick limbs, and translucent skin. Her eyes were the same dull black; indifferent, as they stared back at Martha, and seemingly without malice. But she had changed in one striking respect: the disordered mass of her hair had lengthened and straightened, so that now it framed rather than obscured her face, and it glowed with an odd, captivating light that had nothing to do with the fluorescent tubes in the ceiling above them. *Lustrous* was the word that occurred to Martha. Veronica's hair looked like a model's in some kind of celestial shampoo advert, but there was no suggestion that it was fake. However much it clashed with the waif-like remainder of her, this hair was definitely part of her. In an unsettling way, it even seemed the *realest* part of her.

"What do you want, Veronica?" Martha said.

"I keep telling you. I want to understand."

Veronica drifted away over the silent ward, pausing for a moment above each bed-bound patient. She kept speaking as she went.

"Did you know I was once as high and free as Simon used to be? Of course, I didn't start like that. I started low, and climbed, because I wanted to. Then I tried to climb even higher, but the rulers stopped me. They said it wasn't lawful."

Veronica made a face.

"Simon called me *fallen.* Well, if I fell, I was pushed! And I only ended up back where I started, anyway. Crawling along the bottom. But now, I'm wondering about falling even further. Earth really fascinates me, Martha Mud."

Martha tried hard to make sense of this, but couldn't.

"You're in Air," she said. "You're a Being of Air. This place isn't somewhere you should be. I really don't want you here, Veronica."

"What makes you think *you* belong here? You don't belong anywhere!"

Martha felt the truth of this like the thrust of a knife.

"Look at your body," the girl continued. "Why did you say no to it? It could have been fixed. It could probably still be fixed, if there was something inside it."

Again, Martha was confounded by the girl's words. Only now, Veronica dizzyingly changed tack.

"Is that your brother?" she said.

Martha glanced involuntarily at Mark as he sat by the bed. Almost as if he somehow knew they were talking about him, he now reached forward, and placed his broad fingers over Martha's body's wrist. The hand attached to it didn't react. It might have been made of plasticine instead of bones and sinews and skin.

"You know you can hear them, don't you?" Veronica said. "The humans in Earth. Go up really close to them, and you can hear what they're thinking."

"What?"

"Well, of course. What do you think Air is? What do you think *thinking* is? It happens on the borders of Air and Earth, and then takes wing. Gets a life of its own. Just like my *monster*."

Veronica suddenly dropped down towards the bed. Martha tensed, wanting to claw her back, wanting to shout, but the silence of the hospital ward, and the wrongness of Veronica being there, and all her conflicting emotions, cast a spell that Martha couldn't for a moment shake free of. Paralysed, she watched as Veronica appeared to stand on the floor, just behind Mark's chair. Then she leaned her head close to his ear, and held it there.

It was absolute terror that now gripped Martha. Veronica, though, didn't appear to touch him. She kept perfectly still as she bent over him. After just a few seconds, she rose back and away from him, and returned to Martha's side.

"He isn't very happy," she said. "His head's quite a mess. He's thinking about all kinds of things. He's remembering all kinds of things."

"What have you done?" said Martha.

"I didn't *do* anything! I listened. I just told you. Here on the boundary, you can listen."

"I don't believe you."

Veronica laughed.

"He was thinking about the time he cleaned up your vomit."

"What?"

"So tender, wasn't he? Even though he was so

angry at your mum for just sitting there. He sang you back to sleep."

Martha felt like she wanted to be sick all over again. Could this *thing* really have listened to Mark's thoughts? Was it some kind of trick? Perhaps Veronica was somehow prying into *Martha's* thoughts, creeping inside her and stealing what she found there.

Had Mark sung to her, that night when she'd realised Joan was gone for good? But she couldn't remember. She couldn't remember.

"This is what I mean about Air and Earth," said Veronica. "This is what's so fascinating. Thoughts being mothered and fathered in one element, but then finding they really belong in another. Do you want to know what *I* think, Martha Mud?"

Martha didn't answer her.

"Well, I'll tell you anyway. I think *souls* are the place where Air and Earth meet. You don't just cross borders, you are the border."

PART FOUR

1

Mary takes a long, deep breath, and looks at me like an astronaut might look at an orphaned baby Martian. The compassion is obvious, but so is the incredulity, and the slight twinge of aversion. I drop my own gaze, and rest it in my lap.

"Have you considered writing this down, Martha?" she says. "Your story. All of it. It might help you. And it might help *me,* to read it. I must say, at this point I'm finding it increasingly hard to follow."

"Writing it down?"

No, the idea hasn't occurred to me. To be honest, when I woke up in the hospital, in my body – in how my body now is – I didn't give a great deal of thought to what happened to Martha after she jumped. This might sound unlikely, given the strangeness and the importance of what happened, but I felt right away that the story was over. It had reached its end, and here I was in the present, trying to imagine a new story.

I woke up a long time ago. I was in hospital for months. When I finally got to leave, they made me see a counsellor, and I found myself telling this story that I thought I'd placed firmly in my past, because Mary asked me what I remembered, and I saw no reason not to at least try to give her the truth. And now, Mary's saying I should write it down!

I mull it over.

One thing about being bedridden, it makes you really think about time. When you're flat on your back 24/7, time is endless, and you measure it by an eternal routine of meals, and physio, and the consultants checking up on you. Your life has become miniscule (although Martha's life before she jumped wasn't exactly enormous) – just the four walls of your hospital ward, and your own helpless body – and now you find a whole tsunami of time has rushed in to fill it. If you're not careful, everything gets drowned.

So, you realise you've got choices. Do you blitz out eternity with the opiate of the TV screen? Do you plug yourself in to your laptop: look at porn, trawl through Twitter, subscribe to a zillion YouTube channels? Or do you just sleep, and then stare into space? (Many did, on my ward; although who knows what meds they were on, and who am I to judge them?)

I took to reading. Yes: actual books. I hadn't ever read before, not seriously. But one day as I was lying there, I remembered doing *Romeo and Juliet* at school. It was difficult and long, and in keeping with most of the rest of the class, I was ready to give up almost as soon as I'd started. If it wasn't for my teacher – and the fact that I had to plough through at least some of it if I wanted to pass my GCSE – giving up was also where I would have ended. My teacher was brilliant, though. He was passionate, and knowledgeable, and he had the miraculous trick of aligning himself with this long-dead Elizabethan writer so that both of them, in tandem, somehow drew me in.

I grew to love that play, in the end.

So I started reading Shakespeare. I started trying to teach myself how to read him. Which, after *Romeo and Juliet,* wasn't as hard as I'd thought it could have been.

And when I fancied a change, I started reading everything else.

Result! Eternity was now sentences. Paragraphs and chapters and page numbers, and fresh new book covers. And eternity was fillable, because believe me, the number of books to read is truly endless.

Well. My counsellor's now suggested I write my own book – because I know at once that it's going to take a book to write my story down in.

Not a long book, maybe, but still a book.

I've never really tried writing. But then, I'd never really tried reading, before I did.

If you can read, then you can write.

That's something else I remember my teacher saying, along with a hundred and one things about Shakespeare. I've tried to test out the things he said about Shakespeare, and decided that some of them might have some merit. Maybe I should test this statement out, too, no matter how dumb I always thought it sounded.

"Okay," I tell Mary. "I suppose I could have a go at it."

Mary smiles.

"Good," she says. "Writing can be very therapeutic. And as I say, it might help me understand your story better."

And as *I've* said in this book a number of times, it's to help Mary understand that I'm trying to write it. But do I think it's helping *me?* Do I think it's *therapeutic?*

I told Mary right at the start of our very first session that I didn't need a counsellor, and I said the same thing at the start of this book. For me, the story's ended. *That* story's ended. And living that story was all the counselling I needed.

Probably, if anything's helping me, dear Mary – if anything's making me understand things more clearly – it's writing down all these pieces of my new story. It's writing down you and me.

2

Martha left Veronica, and Mark, and her body, and ranged out into Air. She needed to be alone. She needed time to think.

For a while, she moved restlessly between the limits of the town, from outlying villages to railway tracks to motorway, but although she still couldn't see it, she couldn't shake off the knowledge of what lay above her. And was Simon still up there, too, stuck behind the invisible wall of Veronica's monster?

It occurred to her then that probably, Veronica had allowed her to pass through it. Nothing else could explain why it hadn't torn her to pieces.

She thought about going back to the place Veronica had taken her, to the house by the sea. But picturing it, she couldn't see herself doing anything different from last time. Whether Lionel was really living there or whether he wasn't, his flesh and blood body was lost to her.

She wondered how Joan was coping, when Mark clearly wasn't. She wanted to know, but dreaded finding out. Her brother had been strong, and now he was weaker than water. Her mother had had strength, too, once upon a time, but she'd offered it up to the memory of her husband; and now that her daughter was gone as well, what could she possibly have left?

And through all these thoughts of her family, past and present, ran the helpless refrain: *What can I do?*

Martha moved.

Cold, she thought. *Space.*

Distance.

A cliff of ice plunged below her into blue-black waves. More ice floated on the water in a thousand different shapes and sizes: blocks and plates and swooped-out mountains, spires and pinnacles, domes and arches. They looked so other-worldly! So brilliantly sparkling!

Martha stared, awestruck and humbled. Nothing she'd ever seen in Earth had been this beautiful.

She flew out amongst them, skating between their impossible curves and spikes; taking a small, frozen kind of joy in her agility, and in the privilege of her being where she was, and seeing what she was seeing.

Time passed. In Earth, time passed. She lingered above a blue wedge of ice that sloped into the sea, and watched as the sun spun slowly round the edge of the horizon.

There were no birds. There were no creatures in the water that she could see, and no sign of humans. Martha realised suddenly that this was the first Earth-bound place she'd moved to that held no memory for her; that couldn't possibly have pulled her. Yet as lovely as it was, it was lifeless. It felt like a desert.

I'd be dead of cold by now, she thought, if I was still in my body.

And then, quite out of nowhere, Martha was visited by a hunger for what she'd possessed before she jumped.

This hunger surprised her with its vehemence. It screamed at her. She wanted an intact spine again, so she could sit up in that hospital bed and hug her brother. She wanted to be able to inhabit that plasticine hand and squeeze back. She wanted lips and lungs and larynx to make a voice that could reach him.

What would she say to him? Anything. What did it matter, so long as he heard it? Anything!

Martha had no desire to *be* what she'd been before she jumped, or to go back to the life she'd been living in Earth. If she wanted her body returned to her, it wasn't to taste food with, or drink Chardonnay, or have an orgasm. It certainly wasn't to take it to school, or to sit it on the sofa while her mum beside her did nothing, said nothing, or to drape it on her bed and stare at the artex on her ceiling.

She wanted her body back in order to connect. She wanted it back so that she could be real to someone. Because who could she be real to, where she now found herself?

Phantoms. No-one.

Be and do in Air. That's what she'd been told. But the things she wanted to do could only be done in Earth, and Earth was forever out of her reach.

Why was she here? Why had her angel abandoned her?

You don't belong anywhere, the girl had said.

For an instant, Martha wanted fingers just so she could thrust them into the ice and feel it burn her.

The chunk over which she floated threaded its way between two enormous pillars, heading slowly out to sea. The single span of cliff from which all these oddments of ice must have fallen towered in the near distance, far taller than the pillars, its deep cracks and chasms stealing sunlight.

Martha tried desperately to clutch at what might still be possible. Veronica had claimed to have listened to Mark's thoughts. It was probably a lie, but could Martha go back to the hospital and find out for sure? She imagined leaning close to her brother, just as Veronica had done, and then hearing the words the voice inside him spoke; and as she imagined it, the temptation to try it grew in perfect tandem with the certainty that trying it would be wrong.

Spying on what was happening in someone's else's head. Opening their secrets. Streaming their memories. What a horribly enticing fantasy! No. She just couldn't do it.

And yet Veronica had also said that human souls were the link between Air and Earth. Whatever that really meant, Martha was a human soul; she was nothing else. What if she could somehow use her humanness – and use Mark's, too – to bridge the gap between them? What if she could not only hear, but *speak to* her brother? She wasn't able to touch him, but maybe she could whisper to him.

Whisper anything.

Something was about to shift in the ice shelf in front of her. Martha knew it before it happened. She saw, in Air, that it was so: the shadow of a tremble, a slip, a snapping of bonds. Then, in Earth, she watched as a whole face of the cliff slid away and fell towards the sea. She heard no sound. The splash it made sent a wave as big as houses foaming slowly towards her.

Martha rose, to see her own small wedge covered, and the pillars it had sailed between wading in ocean.

It was time to go back. It didn't matter what Veronica wanted from her. Martha wanted something now, and as she moved, that was all she cared about.

3

Pulled by desires…

Martha found it incredibly strange, telling and then writing her story, that in Air she had craved so many things, one after the other, while during her life in Earth, before she jumped, she hadn't been aware of wanting much of anything at all.

What had she wanted in Air?

To move on her own.

To find her father.

To question her angel.

To gain a shape.

To speak to her brother.

Her desires while in her body had been pale, whimsical, transient things. A boy. A slice of pizza. Not to feel. To be invisible.

Her desires in Air turned out almost as fleeting, but they came from the core of her, and forced her each time to act on them.

Veronica – Martha's friend Veronica, or Ronnie, or

Nika – had self harmed since she was ten. Well, that's what she claimed, although Martha had spent as much time with her at ten as she had at fourteen, which was when Martha first heard about it.

They'd been sitting in Nika's bedroom, and Nika had pulled up her top to show Martha the scars. Martha had stared, fascinated and alarmed. Nika was left-handed, and a hundred tiny silver threads stitched up her skin from the top of her jeans to just below her heart.

Martha had looked at Nika's face, to see if she was bragging. Nika had always been good at bragging: at parading in front of Martha things she couldn't do, or things she didn't have. But no. Nika's face was matter of fact.

"Does anyone else know?" Martha had asked.

"Just you," Nika said.

Martha looked back at the ladder of scars.

"Why?"

"Because sometimes I can't feel, and sometimes I want to. I *really* want to."

Desire came in a million differently wrapped packages, Martha had decided.

Don't get Martha wrong. When she said there was something dark and secret about Veronica, she didn't specifically mean her self harming. The self harming was a symptom, an aspect of it, but not the core of it. Martha still doesn't know what the core of it might have been. She doesn't feel like she ever truly understood her friend, as close as they were; and Martha's never been closer to anyone else.

Yet seeing those scars, Martha was fascinated and alarmed, but she wasn't surprised.

Nika couldn't really have been cutting herself for as long as she said she had. Martha would have seen, would have noticed. Wouldn't she?

She tried to think back.

Nika had always worn a one-piece swimsuit, even in the hottest of weathers in one or other of their back gardens, screaming and spraying each other with the hosepipe. Those naked, tomfoolery sleepovers: how old had they been? But the lights had always been out. That had been half the fun of it.

Changing for gym at school, Nika wore a vest tucked into her pants, and never took it off with her gym shirt, no matter how sweaty it must have got. Martha had assumed modesty, although when Nika dressed for parties – or even just for an afternoon on the high street – she wasn't exactly shy in revealing legs and cleavage.

So perhaps it was true. A ten year old, and a razorblade. Then four years of threading those little stitches into herself. And no one guessing.

Martha's most consistent desire, since Lionel left, had been not to desire anything. There in Nika's bedroom, Nika had got out the razorblade and shown her how she did it. Again, not bragging. Just showing.

"Do you want to try it?" Nika had said.

Martha had looked at the glinting, deceptive edge of what Nika was holding out to her. She tried to imagine it slipping under her skin, and what it would feel like.

"No thanks," she'd replied.

Trying to be as matter of fact as her friend.

Martha thought she knew what it would feel like, and what else it might make her feel. And this was exactly what she *didn't* desire.

Martha hadn't spoken to Nika for three weeks after that. It wasn't to spite her, or to criticise her, although she wondered if Nika might have thought it was. But the episode had shaken Martha's foundations in all kinds of ways, and she'd desperately needed to indulge her own solution, which was blankness, and the shelter of the familiar, and solitude.

Silence.

The knots and whorls on her bedroom ceiling.

Neither Martha nor Nika ever mentioned it again. After Martha went back to talking to her, and all the way on until Nika left for Wales a year later, their friendship ploughed its course as if none of it had happened.

But why had Nika told Martha, when she'd told no one else?

Martha sometimes wishes she'd had the courage to ask her. Nika must have had her reasons, and Martha doesn't believe they were malicious reasons, as capable of malice as she knew Nika was.

More often, Martha wishes that Nika had never told her, and never shown her. And then, she feels guilty. Not guilty for not trying to help, because back then, Martha wouldn't have been able to help if she'd tried.

No. Martha feels guilty for never telling Nika that she understood, and understood perfectly. That she'd refused that blade not out of squeamishness, or disapproval, or bafflement, but out of pure cowardice.

Martha Mud, in Earth, was a coward through and through. She stayed in her room as much as she was able, shut up inside herself; locked away from her own desires as much as she was locked away from the rest of the world and *its* desires.

In Air, Martha Mud found that her desires

were released. She chased them, one after another, forgetting everything else. And she suffered because of them, but it was a very different kind of suffering to what she'd endured when her desires were chained, and bound, and briared.

Once she was dead, Martha started to live; and life kept surprising her.

4

In the blink of an eye – whose eye? – Martha had no eyes – maybe God's, although Martha hadn't yet heard anyone mention such a Being – she was back in the intensive care unit, looking down at what she'd only just started missing.

Veronica wasn't there, and neither was Mark. The nurses were different nurses, and one of the beds that had been filled was now empty.

Someone else sat on the plastic chair by Martha's body. It was a woman. Martha saw her back at first, and didn't recognise her. This back was very upright. She was dressed in a smart grey jacket, and a neat bob of auburn hair fell to her shoulders.

Martha swung around the walls to take a look.

It was Joan. It was Martha's mum.

Martha still nearly didn't recognise her. There was an alertness to Joan's gaze, fixed on her only daughter, that like a hard little stone in a pool sent out ripples through Martha's memory. She gazed as if she was waiting for something.

Waiting for something she was certain would happen, but she didn't know when.

She was wearing make-up. Joan hadn't worn make-up since Martha, and Mark, and Lionel, had all been part of one family.

Martha kept staring, her heart nearly bursting. She couldn't believe what she was seeing. At this same bedside, Mark had looked like he'd fallen to pieces. Joan looked like she'd found all her pieces, and scrubbed and polished them, and glued them together so the cracks were invisible. She was holding Martha's body's hand, just as Mark had done, but her eyes radiated energy. In Air, Martha could see it: like a thunderclap of sun.

What had happened to all those dulled, misty clouds, Martha wondered? Where had they gone?

At last, Joan stood, and bent carefully amongst the tubes and drips to kiss her daughter on the cheek. Then she went over to one of the nurses. She said something brief, and smiled. The nurse smiled back.

Joan left the ward, and Martha lingered for a moment. Her body seemed unchanged. It was just as ruined, just as empty.

Then Martha sucked herself up through the hospital roof, and out into the daylight.

Simon was waiting for her.

The boy looked awful. Like an inversion of her mother, all his grace, all his brilliance, had vanished without a trace.

"The monster's gone," he said. "I don't know where. I'm not going to follow it. Did you talk to Veronica?"

"Yes," Martha said. "She was there in the hospital. But that was a long time ago. I'm sorry, I don't know how long. I went far away. I'm sorry."

Martha was stunned by what she'd just seen in the ICU. A new desire had pushed out all the others, and she couldn't think clearly about anything else.

"What did she say?" asked Simon. "What did she do?"

"Nothing. She talked about Air and Earth. I didn't understand it."

"She means you harm," said Simon.

"I don't care. I don't care about Veronica."

"But she cares about you, human soul. She wants something from you that you won't be able to take back."

"What about what *I* want?" said Martha.

They looked at each other. Simon's eyes were like rocks. Coarse black stubble covered his cheeks.

A tiny part of Martha's heart went out to him; but only a tiny part.

"I'm sorry," she repeated. "I'm going."

Joan was on a bus. It was with a little yelp of delight that Martha found her: this confirmation that she could wish for something, imagine something, and move directly to it.

Her mum sat on the bus seat the same way she'd sat on the hospital chair, ramrod straight, holding her handbag. Her eyes now bore a weight that hadn't been evident in the hospital, but they remained clear and purposeful. Martha positioned herself above the seat in front so she could gawp at her. Joan faced forwards, staring right through her.

After a few stops, Joan got off. They were on the High Street. It was maybe mid morning, judging by the mums with their buggies and the cruising vans, and all the pubs still closed. Joan headed down a side street and went into an office. *Timpson's Solicitors* it said on the window in no-nonsense lettering.

What was she doing in there? Martha hung at a corner of the building opposite, waiting for her mother to come out again. Time passed, but she didn't reappear. Losing patience, Martha slid through the brick and searched for her.

Here Joan was, in a side room, sat at a desk. Her fingers were busy on a keyboard; the desk held files and pieces of paper.

Was it possible? Did her mother have a job?

Joan had gone on long term sick leave after Lionel told her he was staying in America. Then, as prescription piled on prescription and the

177

weeks and months dragged by, she'd moved onto full blown disability. Every so often during the next eight years, the benefit office would push her into finding something, shopwork, or cleaning, or telesales; but she never lasted long.

And now Martha remembered what she'd done when she still had a husband. Legal secretarial. It was what she'd trained for.

Timpson's Solicitors.

Martha was dumbfounded. How had she managed it? For the first time in forever, her mum was clean, and this should have been obvious to anyone who saw her, but to Martha, in Air, Joan was limpid, transparent, a drop of pure water. How had she ditched her meds and then found herself a job, with a history of psychiatric problems and probably no references?

It felt to Martha that she'd lurched into an alternate reality. How much time had passed since Martha had jumped? How long had her body been lying in that hospital?

The door opened, and a man came into the room where Joan sat typing. Joan looked up from the screen, and her face lit up. It was such a normal, human reaction, an impulse of open friendliness, but seeing it made Martha want to cry.

For fully half of Martha's life, her mother had been wrapped in bandages like the Invisible Man. Martha had always been certain that if she pulled aside those bandages, she'd find nothing underneath them.

But look. The bandages were off, and here was her mother: as brightly perceptible as anyone could wish.

Martha withdrew from that room and moved out into the silent street, then up into the Air above it. She watched the shoppers and the idlers and the mobility scooters going to and fro beneath her. She watched as the pubs opened; as the library closed; as buses spilled out passengers, and car parks filled and emptied. So many people. So many lives.

She remembered being above the coastal metropolis with Simon, when she'd given him a name. What had he said, then?

Too many. A pestilence.

Were all these human beings she could see too many?

And yet Joan, her mother, was one of them. And so was her brother.

When Joan left the office, Martha followed her. It looked like she was going home. From the centre of town, it was probably a walk of about twenty minutes. Streetlights were flickering on, and car headlights probed the dusk.

All the trees, Martha noticed, were bare.

There were crocuses and daffodils coming out in people's gardens. What time of year had it been when she'd jumped? Surely it hadn't been spring. Not winter, either.

Joan arrived at the house she'd once shared with her husband and children. There was no car in the drive. Joan had never got her license; never wanted to, she said. Lionel, that multiple license holder, had always laughed.

Joan found her door key and went inside.

Martha twisted above the roof, feeling almost the same as she'd felt when she'd gazed at the whitewashed house by the seashore. Almost, but not quite. The new desire she'd found filled her with hope: that something more might be available to her than being an audience of one at an endless silent movie.

Martha took hold of herself, and plummeted.

The first thing that struck Martha as she came down into the hall was that everything was spotless. She glanced at the stairs, freshly vacuumed, then pushed through the paintwork and into the lounge.

Mark had kept everything pretty tidy while he'd been living here, but when he went, entropy had quickly asserted itself. It was amazing to Martha how dust built up; how stains appeared on kitchen tiles, and empty coffee jars and coins and toast crumbs gathered on surfaces, and clothing draped itself on chairs, and strands of cobweb hung themselves in corners.

Now, the house was like new: not only was it scrubbed, there was so much less *stuff.* The sofa was definitely new, with plumped pastel cushions, and it faced a different wall. The coffee table beside it held only three things: a lamp, an empty coaster, and a framed photograph.

Martha looked at the photograph. Her own face stared back at her. It was a school photo. Martha was vaguely, unwillingly smiling, her body dressed in school uniform.

She went into the kitchen, and found her mother taking the packaging from an oven ready chicken meal. She watched her read the instructions, and stick it in the microwave. She watched her fill a glass of water from the tap, and sip it, and wipe an accidental dribble from her chin. A huge diffidence filled Martha then. It was suddenly all too personal. She felt like a voyeur.

She went back into the lounge – this changed, stranger's room – and crouched beneath the curtains.

When her mother had finished eating and had cleaned away her things, she sat back down at the dining table, and turned on her laptop. Her eyes took in the screen in almost the same way that they'd watched her daughter's body in the hospital.

Martha hung behind her, and saw what she saw.

There were web pages about head injuries, and spinal injuries, and tracheostomies, and home ventilation. About charities and grants. About prognoses, and survival rates. Page after page. And Joan kept scrolling doggedly through all of it, with that look of patient expectancy illuminating her gaze.

Martha could bear her own wait no longer. This was what she'd come for. This was what she'd imagined trying with her brother, there above the ice floe. She didn't care if it was lawful. She just needed to know if it could be done.

She bent to this human being, just as Veronica had bent to Mark in the ICU, and then she heard what she heard, and said what she said.

5

"Hang on a minute. Are you telling me you listened to your mother's thoughts?"

Mary's asked this question partly in open disbelief, and partly, paradoxically, in outright censure.

But I'm not about to take any blame for this.

"Yes," I say. "I spoke to her, too."

"You spoke to her?"

"Yes."

"What did you say? Do you feel able to tell me, Martha?"

Except now I'm suddenly stumbling. Of course, I've always known this part of my story was coming. When it actually arrived, I'd imagined myself maintaining a mysterious silence. And that says it all: not a *principled* silence.

So I say:

"I know it wasn't right. Thoughts are private, aren't they? Thoughts that aren't directed at you."

"Directed?"

"Well, of course. Everyone hears thoughts all

the time. We're human souls. We're a part of Air. That's how things are."

Now I've lost her. Mary stares at me, and for an instant, she lets slip a look of something like annoyance.

Dear Mary.

"Haven't you ever *known* that somebody's thinking about you?" I say. "You think of them, and they answer. You can think of a hundred different people, and nothing comes back to you. Then you think of someone who's doing the same, and suddenly you're in a hot spot. You've got a connection."

Mary doesn't reply, but I can see she's making an honest attempt at making sense of what I'm saying.

"That's basically what being in love is, isn't it?" I say.

"Being in love?" says Mary. She shakes her head. "Martha, I'm not sure anyone really knows what being in love is. Not even me, and I've got a psychology degree."

"Being in love – well, yes, it's probably lots of things – but part of it is sending and receiving thoughts about each other, which happens in Air. Passionate, compulsive thoughts, obviously. But isn't that what all those songs talk about? *Even though you're far away,* or however they all go?"

"Not necessarily," says Mary. "I think it's possible to be in love with someone, and to miss them very badly, even when you're pretty sure they aren't thinking of you at all."

"But that's why it hurts so much," I say. "You're sending, but you're not receiving. You're getting nothing back."

Mary frowns, and tilts her head at me slightly.

"And what about when you find yourself thinking of someone," I continue, "and the very next second they send you a text or give you a call? Well, that's Air. That's what Air is. That's how Air works."

Now my counsellor laughs.

"I'm sure almost everyone's had that experience, Martha, and there's always the temptation to imagine it's more than just chance. But chance is all it is."

"What's chance?" I say. "I mean really, what *is* chance? Isn't it just a way of scientists saying they can't predict something? That they don't actually know what the hell's going on? Isn't it just a convenient myth?" I snort; not a pretty sound, probably. "If you believe in chance, you might as well believe in angels."

Mary looks baffled.

"Chance is just... chance."

She sighs; scratches her neck; takes off those glasses and starts wiping them. Wow. Double whammy!

"Okay," she says. "Think about clouds, Martha. Random collections of water droplets. But when we look at them, we see animals. Faces.

Dragons and camels and giants. Human beings are always searching for some kind of meaning – that's how we are – and even when it really isn't there, we insist on projecting it."

And there it is: she's picked *this* particular example, out of anything else she might have chosen. I can't quite believe she's being that obtuse; that outright insensitive.

"No," I say.

But now, Mary's giving me her slightly sorrowful, compassionate, patronising look.

"I might not be able to tell you what being in love is," she says, "but this is what I *do* know. When we're emotionally involved in a situation, it can be very difficult to see it clearly. To see it for what it really is, and not make wrong assumptions about it, and jump to wrong conclusions."

"I'm not jumping to anything," I snap back at her. "Quite honestly, Mary, I've had enough of jumping. Look, I've read so much since I woke up, and so much of it makes sense to me. Writers who sound like they know what I know. It's all out there. And really, it's all obvious, if you open your eyes."

"What's obvious, Martha?"

"That what schools and colleges and universities teach about how the universe works is only a tiny part of the story. We've put the universe in a box. How have we all decided that the universe can fit in a box?"

"I don't think what gets taught in schools is a

box, exactly," begins Mary; but I interrupt her.

"What *I* got taught was a load of nonsense. When I turn on the TV, it's all nonsense. When I look around, and see how everyone lives their lives —"

But I stop, abruptly. I've got angry, and I've realised that the more I keep talking, the more crazed and incomprehensible I'm going to start sounding.

Mary, though, looks genuinely apologetic. In fact, she looks mortified.

"I'm sorry, Martha," she says. "I really didn't mean to start arguing with you. I don't know what came over me."

I probably huff a little at this point, and stare at the floor.

"It's my job to listen, and I'm not doing it very well, am I?" Mary says.

"I'd like to go on with the story now," I say. "If you want to hear it."

"Yes, please, Martha. You were telling me about your mother, and how you…"

"Yes," I say. "My mother. I listened to her thoughts, and then felt bad for doing it. And then I told her something."

To do her justice, Mary, at this point, allows me some silence. When she's sure I'm not going to fill it, she says:

"But you don't feel comfortable disclosing what it was."

"No," I say.

Mary sighs deeply, and the counselling room goes quiet again. If the clock on the desk wasn't digital, we'd have heard it ticking. And now I can see Mary struggling with herself. She's got a question she really wants to ask, but she's trying to foresee all the possible consequences of asking it before she commits herself.

Maybe she's decided that on balance, it's okay. Or maybe – although I can't imagine she'd admit it – it's just her curiosity winning out.

"Does your mother remember this?" she says. "Does she remember hearing you speak to her?"

"I never asked her," I say. "I didn't need to."

Paradigm shift is one of the best concepts I've come across while I've been reading. If you look back through history, at any one part of it, people have generally thought the same kinds of things. There's an energy to the ideas they hold collectively that's enormously hard to break. But sooner or later, like a crack in a dam, a different idea starts taking hold of us, and then suddenly it breaks everything wide open. The way we picture ourselves changes. The way we live changes. The way we die changes.

Then things get walled up again. Until the next new idea appears...

Whatever we believe now, about almost anything: in a hundred, a thousand years – maybe even ten! – it's a given that we'll look back, and say our old beliefs were limited. Mistaken. Ignorant. Deranged.

And yet we all still hold on to our everyday ways of thinking, looking only derisively at our past, complacently at our present, and imagining that while the future will undoubtedly bring us *more* knowledge, the kinds of knowledge that we'll get, and the ways in which we get it, won't ever change.

Can you imagine that everything you think about the world, and every assumption on which you base the way you live in the world, will one day be held to be wrong? Can you?

But I didn't say any of this to Mary, there in the counselling room. And I didn't say this, either:

I listened to my mother's thoughts. Veronica was right. They were a thing, in Air. They lived and breathed in Air. It was like smelling her perfume, or kissing her skin.

Come back to me, she said.

And more, a whole lot more that I shouldn't have listened to. That I'm ashamed I listened to.

And then I spoke to her. And I found that my hope, my desire, was right: I could speak without a voice, and my mother could hear me.

I'm sorry, Mary. I'm sorry for not being open with you. But here I am, right now, wide open.

And I've changed my mind about telling you what I said to her.

    I said:

    I'm going to try and come back to you, mum. Somehow – whatever it takes – I'm going to try and come back.

6

Martha's dad and Martha's brother had an uneasy kind of relationship. Lionel didn't have any kids when he got together with Joan, so it must have been very strange and new and inevitably difficult suddenly acquiring an eight year old stepson. He had no history with this kid; hadn't been around to change nappies, or watch him learn to walk, or buy him his first bike. And buried in the kid's history was the tragic death of his biological father.

At least there'd been no interfering ex to worry about.

And then, pretty soon afterwards, Lionel's own child came along. A daughter. And Lionel could now change nappies, and be present for all the milestones, and buy her anything he wanted.

But meanwhile, the step-kid was still there: withdrawn, and different, and often unapproachable, and accelerating towards puberty, when even blood parents tend to lose their sons and daughters, until they decide they want to come back again.

Is it possible to love two children equally,

but one that isn't yours? Martha doesn't know. She thinks, she hopes, that love of any kind whatsoever is always possible. That's how humans are. But she's pretty sure that Lionel never managed to love Mark as much as he loved her.

Love in any family is such a tangled, intricate web of connections. There are strands that are weaker, and strands that are stronger. Sometimes the weak links end up damaging the stronger ones. The strong links can galvanise the weak links, or strain them to breaking point. And nothing in love stays constant. Nothing. What's strong becomes weak. What's weak becomes strong.

(Lionel, of course, found a love outside the web – whether it was freedom, or motorbikes, or another human being doesn't really matter – and that left-field link snapped everything, in the end. But anyway…)

Here they all were. A family. Four human souls, different ages, different sexes, different genetic relationships: all woven together by more or less of love.

Martha, of course, can only guess what went on as she was growing up. When she was a toddler, she knew the love of her dad, and for her dad, as an all-consuming thing that blinded her to how other parts of the web might have been sagging. But her mum's love was never in doubt, and she worshipped her brother, and it felt like he loved her. The web held her safe, and that's all she was able to care about.

She remembers, though, when she first saw that Lionel and Mark were having problems even liking each other.

It was her sixth birthday. Yes – the one with that scooter. Martha was an August baby, it was a bright sunny day, and the plan for the morning was going to the park. Mark would have been thirteen. His birthday was in November.

Mark had been there to watch her unwrap her presents. Martha doesn't remember what he got her. But then he'd disappeared, while Lionel and Joan fussed around her, and gave her sweets, and held out the promise of birthday cake later. The park was Lionel's idea, and of course, everyone was going.

Martha remembers struggling with shiny new boots: another present. And then she remembers hearing shouting, and banging on a door. Then Lionel marched into the lounge dragging Mark by the scruff of his neck.

"You're coming!" Lionel had yelled. He was furious. "Jesus Christ, it's your sister's birthday! You're coming!"

Martha had looked at her brother, and her brother had looked at Martha. Martha remembers that look. Some sights, some sounds, are tattooed on your memory: they're never coming off again. As plain as a thought in Air, Mark's look said:

This man is your father. I don't love you less because of him. But I hate your father. I hate him.

Well. That's what can happen. And two years

193

later, Lionel left.

Martha doesn't think Mark hated Lionel for the whole of the time they lived together, and she knows that Lionel at least tried to love her brother, as much as he was able. She has other memories. But this one link was weak, and Joan's love for all of them didn't seem able to make it any stronger.

As I've said a number of times, Martha never really knew her brother, any more than she really knew Joan or Lionel. She lived with them, and loved and was loved by them, and she saw with mostly clear eyes lots of different sides to them. But then out of the blue, each of them showed her another side that she'd never suspected they had. Lionel left. Joan closed down. Even Mark spilling his guts out on Suicide Bridge had left her with questions and no answers; questions to which the only answer she could imagine was jumping.

These other, inexplicable sides to the people she cared about weren't sides you could see through, they were blank, brick walls.

7

After Martha had spoken to her mother, she went to find Simon. She moved herself back to the stone circle on the hill, and hoping that Veronica wouldn't follow her there, she called him.

Simon didn't come for a long time.

As she waited for him, Martha thought about all the things she'd been and done since she fell up into Air. She'd refused her body. She'd refused to drift, too, and learned how to move. She'd tried to find her angel, and been told to find a shape instead. She'd given names to two Beings: Simon and Veronica.

She'd tried to find her father, and perhaps she had, but she'd lacked the courage to see the job through.

She'd discovered that her brother was falling apart without her.

She'd discovered that her mother had somehow become whole again without her, and she'd trespassed into Earth to talk to her.

Finally, she'd made a decision: to do everything in her power to fall *down* again, and go home.

She still wasn't sure if this was the right decision. She still wasn't sure if she was brave enough to actually do it. She'd said no to her body for a reason, hadn't she?

But she'd said no to her angel, too. She'd said no to being dragged up into heaven, or wherever the hell her angel had wanted to take her. Surely there had to be a reason for that, as well.

So what did she need?

A shape, a skin of Air, to protect her from the gale. Then she had to face the dragon and the hurricane, and call her angel back to her.

Would her angel answer? Would her angel consent to return her to her body? Was it even in its power to do so?

But these were questions that couldn't be answered. One step at a time, Martha told herself.

A shape.

Did she have one?

Martha tried to see herself, but couldn't. She remembered stretching out ghostly arms that had melted into waves, but there was nothing to stretch now, and no way of looking at it. Air held no mirrors.

Had she changed since those terrible winds had almost extinguished her?

A purpose ought to have given her a shape, and right now, she had one; but really, she'd been lurching from purpose to purpose ever since she got here.

Deeds ought to have given her a shape too, but hadn't her deeds all been thoughtless, or misguided, or at least inadvertent? Simon had been constant and kind – *acted her angel,* he'd said – and she'd taken him for granted, and changed him in a way she didn't understand, and made him miserable. Against his advice, she'd struck a bargain with Veronica, and changed her as well. And what about communicating with her mother? Had that been the right thing to do? Perhaps she'd held out the hope of something to Joan that wasn't going to be possible.

Probably, talking to Joan had been what Simon would call breaking the rules. It was Veronica, after all, who'd prompted her to try it. She'd felt horribly uncomfortable doing it; she'd felt on a knife-edge of wrong and right. Simon, she was sure, wouldn't have approved.

Martha called him again, but she got no answer. She understood now what his assenting to her call would feel like, and knew he hadn't heard her. It was almost evening, with an orange sun burning in a cauldron of cloud. She ducked towards the stones and came to rest in the middle of them. Their shadows slanted all around her: luminously black on the rabbit-nibbled grass.

She imagined it was too late for hikers now, high up on this hill; but if someone came, Martha knew she had the ability to slip into the space between Air and Earth and listen to their thoughts. The idea was unsettling. She could do it to any one of the billions of people living their lives in that solid realm beneath her. She could do it to Lionel. She could do it to the leaders of the free world, and the leaders of the unfree, if there was really that much of a difference, and whisper peace to them, or whisper war.

She could torment someone with her whispering, if she chose. Drive them mad: hearing not voices, but just one voice: hers.

Could Veronica speak thoughts into someone too, she wondered? This idea was terrifying. And if she could, had she always been able to do it? Or was it a power Veronica had been given when Martha named her?

If her deeds were shaping her, Martha was suddenly fearful of what that shape might be. Surely there was just as much scope in Air for mischief, for evil, as ever there'd been in Earth.

Martha watched as the sun boiled away to nothing, and innumerable stars appeared. How odd, she thought, that as far away as she'd been told those stars were, the reaches of Air were much wider. And Water, and Fire, and whatever was beyond. How odd that humans pointed telescopes and imagined they saw distance, when all the real distances lay in quite different directions.

The universe is wonderfully strange, thought Martha Mud.

And how difficult it is to be a human soul in any part of it.

Simon came with the sun, and like the sun. Martha, still within the circle of stones, was dazzled when he appeared before her.

He'd grown up. He was a young man, furiously beautiful. And he was laughing.

"I didn't understand," he said. "When I offered to help you, and was abandoned. When I felt the Earth in you alter me, and leech all the strength from me. I thought I was lost!"

"What happened?" Martha asked.

She was staggered by the sight of him. He was what he'd been when Martha had first met him, but *more,* and far brighter.

His eyes danced over her, watching her see him.

"Lots has happened," he said. "A whole age has passed since we last talked."

"What do you mean?" said Martha. "It was days ago. Just days!"

"Days for you, perhaps, an age for me. You're still tied to Earth, Martha Mud. But I've been far, and suffered, and triumphed. An age has passed, and everything is new."

"You're new," she said. "You've changed again. You're... *stunning.*"

"Change is what we are. We melt, and shift, and vanish, and appear again. Haven't you learned anything?"

Simon was still laughing.

"But you were so unhappy," she said. "You got so drab and grey. You said it was my fault."

"It was. But I thought you'd changed my nature. I thought I was corrupted. Cast down. I was wrong."

"I shouldn't have named you," Martha said.

"I let you. But now, I have a new name."

Martha stared in surprise.

"What is it?" she asked.

"A Being gave it me. A Being not of Air. But I'm sorry, human soul. I cannot tell you. It wouldn't be lawful."

Simon – what else could she call him? – looked hilariously grave as he told her this. Then he shook his head like a stallion, as if feeling the power of the new name inside him, and stars leapt from his hair in a silver cascade.

"Well, I'm glad," said Martha. "I know you took a risk, helping me. I know you stuck your neck out."

"But you released me, and I'm grateful."

"Released you?"

"You left me three times," said Simon. He looked at her strangely. "Don't you remember?"

"No," said Martha.

"Yes. Once, twice, and the third time broke it. Then I was free of you, and free of Earth."

Left him? Was Simon right? She'd moved to Suicide Bridge, just to show him she could move, which was when she'd met Veronica. She'd plunged down into the monster, when Simon had said, *Don't.* And then she'd left him hanging above the hospital, acned and abject, to follow her mother.

"Oh," said Martha.

And then: "Oh!"

Suddenly understanding that this radiant Being was saying *he* was now leaving *her.*

"I've come to give one final warning. I've given it before. Don't trust what you've named Veronica. Never doubt her ill will, and never doubt her ability to harm you. She wants to be and do in Earth. She wants your body, Martha Mud."

"What?"

"She'll use you to get it. She'll trick you into giving it."

"My *body?* How do you know? I don't understand."

Simon smiled.

"An age has passed. I confronted her, but she was stronger. She boasted. Then she threw her monster at me, and I and the monster fought. How we raged! What a furious battle! But I was gifted. I was graced. I overcame it, and hurled it high, and the winds of Upper Air devoured it."

Martha tried to imagine what Simon had just told her, but she couldn't. She remembered what had sprawled above those mountains. Nothing could ever make her forget it.

"Wow," she said. "That's...wow."

But Simon seemed to radiate both purpose

and complacency. She saw he was ready to be gone.

"So what do I do now?" she said.

Please don't leave me, was what she wanted to say. Martha had a feeling of vertigo, as if events were accelerating out of her control.

Just us. Isn't that what they'd told each other?

Simon eyes radiated kindliness.

"Find your shape and call your angel. And deal wisely with Veronica."

"That's what I'm trying to do," Martha said. "I'm trying to be wise. I've found my mother, and my brother. I want to go back. I want to get back into my body."

I want to hug Mark. I want to rediscover my mum.

"That's good, human soul. There's nothing for you in Air but regret, and confusion, and finally decay. Go back into Earth, if your angel allows it."

"Yes, but how will I know when I'm ready?" said Martha, in something of a panic. "I've been, and done. Do I have a shape? Look at me! What do you see?"

Simon looked.

"An egg," he said. "A spark from a firework that's yet to be lit. A bud."

Then, the Being of Air really did leave her. With a smile that felt like all the combined smiles of everyone Martha had ever loved in her life in Earth, he vanished into the morning, and Martha was alone again.

8

"So do you want to try and tell me what happened to you on that bridge?" says Mary.

We're a long way into the story by now, and we're a long, long way into getting to know each other. I've lost count of the number of times I've been here with my counsellor, in her room in the CAMHS unit, trying my best to explain things to her. But I still haven't talked about the beginning of Martha's story – the story before the story – and we both know I can't keep putting it off forever.

The problem isn't with Mary, or how I imagine she'll interpret what I tell her. The problem is with trying to remember who I once was.

"Mark texted me," I say. "I've told you this before. I hadn't seen him for months, it was out of the blue. He said he needed to talk to me, and he told me where he was."

"Suicide Bridge," says Mary. "That's what people call it, isn't it?"

"Yes," I say.

"How did that make you feel? I mean, that

that was where he wanted to meet you?"

"It didn't make me feel anything. I didn't connect it. Why would I?"

"Okay," says Mary. "I'm sorry. Why don't you just tell me what happened, and I'll just listen."

"Okay," I say.

It had been a really shitty day. It was our first week back at school after the summer holidays – our GCSE year, I'd turned sixteen the month before – and Mr Reynolds, my science teacher, had yelled at me for dropping a test tube full of some sort of acidic gunk that he'd given us to look at. He'd heated it up in a demonstration on his bench, and then passed it to the dutiful row of kids sat on stools in front of him.

"Hold it at the top," he'd said.

At least, that's what I assume he said, but I wasn't listening. I don't know what I was thinking about. Certainly not chemistry. So when my neighbour passed it to me, I grabbed it at the bottom, and scorched my fingers, and the test tube full of gunk smashed and splattered by my feet. And Mr Reynolds had yelled like it was *him* who'd burnt himself. Which I thought was incredibly unfair of him.

Health and safety?!

The clocks hadn't gone back yet, they wouldn't for a while, and the September sun was still warm and redolent of vanished holidays when we made it out of school. My blistered fingers were throbbing. Then I got Mark's text.

Meet me at the bridge. We need to talk.

Suicide Bridge was quite a distance out of my way, but if my brother wanted to see me, I for sure wanted to see him. I bought a bag of chips on the High Street, then threaded through side streets and alleyways onto the common, and started to climb.

We need to talk.

An odd way of putting it. As if we'd had some sort of argument, and now it was time to make up. As if it wasn't *him* who needed to talk. But I didn't really dwell on it, not then.

It was probably around four o'clock when I got there, but the cycle track was empty. I stepped out onto it, and walked to the middle of the bridge. Where was he?

Then I looked through the metal railings, and saw Mark sitting on the parapet.

"Oh my God, what the hell are you doing?" I said. "Come back! That's so insanely dangerous!"

And I stop. Mary's looking at me. The blinds are drawn, and her room's in shadow. It's a safe little cocoon in here, filled with the scent of the roses in a vase on her desk. I don't know why she's got roses. Maybe another client gave them to her. Maybe they're from a husband, or an admirer; except I don't even know if Mary has a husband.

I just sit there glumly, staring back at her, and wondering why I can't go on.

"She climbed down to him," I say.

"I'm sorry?" says Mary.

"Martha Mud went back to the end of the bridge, and pushed through the barbed wire, and edged out above the drop so she could sit with her brother. What else could she do, when she could see straight away what kind of a state he was in?"

Mark's bear of a body sagged over that long fall below both of them, his gaze between his toes. For a long time, he wouldn't look at her. Martha was just inches away from him, but she was frozen with panic, thinking if she moved the slightest muscle towards him, he'd lean forwards and drop.

"You can't mean it," she said.

"I don't know," Mark said. "I can't think of anything else to do."

"You could do anything. Anything but this!"

How had she never realised he was gay? How had she never noticed? That had been the start of the long, snarled up story he'd told her as they sat together. The girlfriend neither she nor Joan had ever met was a boyfriend. And that shouldn't have been any kind of reason to want life to stop, except that Mark seemed to have turned the secrecy of it into something difficult and bad, which was wrong of him, and stupid. Martha loved him. Joan loved him. Perhaps it had been something to do with Lionel.

But the story got harder.

Martha had trouble trying to piece it together, because it was all such a crazy mess, and because the story was just so difficult to relate to this man she thought she knew. The boyfriend had been a boyfriend since Mark was almost thirteen. Three whole years before Lionel left, Martha realised. Then at fifteen, the boyfriend had got into drugs. At seventeen, he was sofa surfing, and stealing, and using junk, while Mark was trying to be a conscientious photography student at college. But Mark hadn't given up on him. He'd kept seeing him, and kept telling him he cared about him, even when this boyfriend probably couldn't even hear him through the fuzz.

Eventually, Mark got him on a methadone program. Held his hand as he slowly straightened out.

And all of this, Martha thought, while Mark was still home every night, cleaning up, and cooking tea, and reading Martha bedtime stories.

That stage of it had come to a close five years ago. The boyfriend had turned himself around completely. He got a good job, and a car, and a flat. Mark had redeemed him. Mark had been his angel.

Then Mark had moved in with him, finally leaving behind him that other piece of wreckage he hadn't been able to make good again: his mum.

This, for Martha, was the period of Mark's irregular flying visits, and having even less of an idea of what made her brother tick than she'd had when they still lived together.

Next came those few months of silence, when Mark seemed to have just vanished, or at least become reduced to the odd little text. *How's it going, little sis.* It seemed the boyfriend had started using again, and Mark was furious with him. He'd tried so hard to save him. He'd *fought* to save him. And now this!

Except there was someone else in the mix, too: someone from the boyfriend's past. A dealer. *His* dealer, now, apparently.

As they talked together on the bridge, Mark told Martha what had happened on that very day, just hours ago: the reason they were both sitting there, high above a gorge on a rusty little ledge.

A little before lunchtime, Mark went home to the flat he'd been sharing with his boyfriend for the last four years. There were perks to being a newspaper photographer, and flexitime was one of them. He parked his car, and climbed the stairs. Stuff was littered all over the floor in the corridor outside the flat's front door. It wasn't even in boxes. It was books and clothes and drawings. It was Mark's books and clothes and drawings. A plastic bag sagging on the top step had Mark's toothbrush and photos and ornaments inside it.

Mark tried his key, but it wouldn't turn.

He said he started hammering on the door then, beating it with his fists. Mark's fists weren't easy things to ignore. After a while, the flat door opened, still on its chain, but the face in the gap wasn't Mark's boyfriend's.

This guy calmly told Mark to get lost, and to take his stuff with him. They'd changed the locks, he said. They'd call the police if Mark wanted trouble. (This, from a drug dealer, with who knows how much stuff stashed in the flat behind him.) No, the boyfriend wasn't interested in talking to him. This was a *clean break,* he said. Now, *fuck off.*

Clean. Mark, on the bridge, had barked a laugh.

What could Mark do? The flat wasn't his. Everything was in his boyfriend's name, the rent, the council tax, even the Netflix.

Mark loved his boyfriend. He'd spent eleven years loving him.

Mark had kicked his own possessions down the stairs, and then left them there at the bottom and gone to find his car.

"Wow," says Mary.

I don't think it's a word I've heard her say before. It sounds odd, coming out of her mouth. She's said it in a small, flat kind of way, as if she's surprised herself by saying it.

"So the boyfriend and this dealer...?" she asks.

"Well, yes. I presume so," I say. "I mean, why else would he have moved in? But Martha didn't ask."

"Oh, my. That's..."

But she doesn't know how to finish this sentence, and neither do I.

Mark was a gentle giant. He was a gentle, gay, wonderful colossus, and to hug him was to be swallowed up in something very solid, and very soft. Martha knows he could have battered down the door and battered down the dealer, and battered down his cheating, using boyfriend too, if he'd have wanted. But he didn't. He walked away, and started battering himself down instead.

That was what she saw quite clearly, as they sat together over that horrible drop. He was thumping away with those enormous fists of his, and whatever substance of himself he was thumping was on the verge of caving in.

Martha was in a predicament. Martha knew she had to do something.

My dictionary defines *predicament* as a disagreeable or dangerous situation. But this word comes from the verb *predicate,* which means to assert that something's true. These two ideas don't at first sight have much of a connection, until you realise that the predicament you're in is disagreeable or dangerous – and mine was both – because your situation's made up of facts, and those facts are inescapable.

That's why Martha jumped from Suicide Bridge: because she looked all the facts squarely in the face, and came to the conclusion that she only had one course of action. Their lives had put Mark and Martha in a cage, and jumping was the only way she could see to break both of them out of it.

But Mary's still sitting there watching me. She hasn't looked at her clock once in the last fifty minutes. She's waiting for me to continue.

PART FIVE

1

Martha felt bereft without Simon. She couldn't believe he'd left her on her own. He'd been the only dependable thing she had.

She wondered if she should have begged him not to go, but it would have been like asking a gale to stop blowing. She'd released him. Her own casual faithlessness had released him.

Not our problem, the rulers in Air had said.

Well, now Martha Mud was strictly her own problem.

Surely it had been a very peculiar kind of miracle that he'd come to her in the first place, and guided her, and been there for her. If a miracle appears for you, how can you reproach it for not staying?

Martha saw clearly that now, the only help she could hope for would come from within: from the shape she was making.

A bud, he'd said.

Martha abandoned the stone circle, and returned to her home town. She'd decided to face up to Veronica. Simon had told her to deal with Veronica wisely; and Martha had the feeling that whatever shape she was going to find for herself, its strength would depend more than anything on how she handled this pitiful, powerful creature.

Martha had named her. They were bound together.

She moved, and it was late afternoon. She was near the park where Lionel had taught her to ride her scooter, and she could see streams of school kids in their uniforms flooding the pavements and eddying through the park gates. How had the sun climbed and fallen so quickly, she wondered? It had been dawn when she'd left the stones.

She found a clump of trees in the middle of the park, beech and plane and chestnut, and poised herself in the Air above them.

Then she called.

Martha wasn't sure if Veronica would answer. Simon had said that named Beings only came if they wanted to. But it seemed Veronica did want to. Air parted its curtains, and with a little swish of an entrance, there she was.

"Hello, Martha Mud," she said. "What do you think? Me and my name have been getting to know each other."

She hung a little distance away with a tiny self-satisfied grin on her face, twirling slightly. Martha could see at once that she'd altered. Her dress had become a garment of clean, lucent yellow. Martha thought of the daffodils she'd seen as Joan had walked home from her new job. Her skinny body was the same, but her hair was longer than ever, and glossier. And her eyes weren't black any more, they were violet. Such jewel-like eyes in such a pallid face were frightening.

Veronica was looking back at her with something like pity.

"Still stuck here, and still shapeless," she said. "You're not going to attract any angels like *that*."

"Simon told me you want my body," Martha said. "Well, you can't have it. It's mine."

Veronica looked puzzled, and amused, and sceptical.

"Really?" she said. "Why would he tell you that?"

"Why can't you just be honest?" said Martha. "You told me in the hospital about how you wanted to fall into Earth. I still don't know how you think that's possible, but I know it's what you want. And you're going to use me, somehow, and use the fact that I named you."

"But why would I want your body? It's broken. It isn't even breathing."

"I don't know," Martha said. "How would I know why you want it? I don't know what you are. I can't work you out. But Simon – "

"*Simon* was wrong. The shell you rejected doesn't interest me. Listen, human soul."

With a swiftness and ferocity that Martha was powerless to defend herself against, Veronica swooped towards her and enveloped her. All Martha could see was a blinding vortex of yellow. She tried to break free, but Veronica held her tight.

"I'm stronger than you, and cleverer than you. I'm ages old. If I wanted your body, I'd make you hand it over. I'd ask you for it nicely, and you'd say yes."

Martha shuddered backwards. Veronica had let her go. She felt like she'd almost been squeezed to nothing.

Veronica's violet eyes bored into her.

"I don't mean you any harm, Martha Mud, but Simon meant *me* harm. He tried to destroy me. Did he tell you that?"

"Yes," Martha said.

"He was your guide. He was your angel. Do *you* mean me harm, Martha Mud?"

"No!" said Martha. "No."

"Good," Veronica said.

She swung away through the bare crown of a chestnut tree, her black hair streaming behind her. Martha quivered where she was, trying to compose herself. What kind of wisdom was she bringing to this meeting, she wondered helplessly? Veronica seemed to just keep running rings around her. *She means you harm.* Those had been Simon's words, and how Veronica had warped them!

"Look," said the girl.

She was pointing at something underneath the trees. Two school kids, a girl and a boy, were walking into the thick of them, hand in hand. Martha didn't recognise them. They were about her own age, maybe a year younger. The girl was lagging behind a little, giggling, the boy pulling her on.

"If I wanted a body," said Veronica, "I'd have one of those. Warm and vital and beautiful. Not smashed up and cooling on a hospital bed."

The girl and the boy reached the middle of the stand of trees, and started kissing. Veronica stared intently at them.

"Feeling your blood move," she said, very quietly. Martha barely heard her. "All those emotions, buried in flesh..."

Veronica swung back towards her.

"Listen, Martha Mud. You said you don't know what I am. I've already given you bits and pieces, but not the whole story. Do you want to hear the rest of it?"

"Okay," Martha said.

She'd once told Simon that she wanted to understand this creature. A woebegone child. A liar. An urchin that could master demons. Now,

Martha still wanted to understand her, but not out of curiosity.

"Simon never guessed what I am, but that's not surprising. There aren't any more of me. I'm entirely unique."

"How?" Martha asked.

"Once upon a time, I was in Earth. I had a body. I had a name, too – a different name – but I lost it. Now I don't even remember it."

Veronica had had a body? Was it possible?

"I chose to give up my name and give up my body, and come up into Air."

"Why?" said Martha.

"Because I was dissatisfied with the constraints I'd been given, and with the life I was told I had to lead. But *dissatisfied* is the wrong word. I *raged* against it."

Rage. Martha had a sudden recollection of the pull of her heart skywards, and her furious urge to say no to it.

"I abandoned my body while it still lived, just like you," said Veronica. "I entered Air and drifted, like you, and learned how to move, like you. And then I discovered what power I had."

"I don't understand," said Martha. "Are you a *soul?*"

"Once," said Veronica. "Perhaps. Not now. I've been in Air too long. After all those ages, I'm Air through and through."

Martha watched, aghast, as Veronica's face twisted. Unshed tears burned in her eyes.

"I thought a name would tell me what I am. It's certainly made me stronger. I know I could climb again, if I wanted, and challenge the rulers again, if I wanted. I know I could become a Queen of Air, if I wanted."

"But you don't," Martha said.

"You told me to tell you the truth. It's this. You're partly right, Martha Mud: I *do* desire a body. I want to return into Earth. I want to be alive again."

Martha was trembling with fear.

"Then call your angel," she said.

"I can't. I never had one."

"What?"

"I never had an angel. I told you I was unique. But ever since I met you, I've been wondering if *you* can be my angel. And now you've given me a name, I bet I can be yours. We can help each other. We can get back into Earth together."

Below them, under the trees, the girl broke away from the boy and darted out towards the grass. There was no sound, of course, but it looked like the girl was laughing. Then suddenly, she fell. She tripped over a tree root and sprawled into a holly bush, both arms extended, her school bag flying. The boy helped her to her feet, consternation on his face. The girl wasn't laughing any more. She was holding up her palms, where tiny spots of red had started welling.

Martha watched Veronica as this small drama played itself out beneath them. All the grief had vanished from her face in an instant. Veronica now looked at the girl with naked craving.

"That's what I want," she murmured. "Skin, and the nerves inside it. I want to *feel*."

2

Martha's body, at sixteen, which was the age it was when it broke, was five foot seven. It had straight, brown, shoulder length hair, and freckles on its arms, and a birth mark on its stomach in the shape of a banana. Its eyes were blue, its nose was sharp, its mouth was small. Its waist was thicker than it could have been, and its thighs chubbier. Its left foot pointed out to the side just a little when it walked.

Martha's body liked salt and vinegar crisps. It liked swimming, but not running. It loved winter cold on its cheeks, and snowflakes in its eyelashes. It hated period pains, and early mornings, and being tickled by anyone but her brother, and too-hot baths.

Martha's body seemed to work okay, most of the time. It didn't have asthma and had never known nicotine, so it breathed pretty well. (It certainly didn't need a ventilator!) It seemed to be able to competently digest almost anything it was fed, although it once rebelled (very messily) at peach schnapps. Its menstrual rhythms were regular. Its eyes could see without glasses. Its skin suffered occasionally from a mild kind of eczema, and hay fever afflicted it most summers, often worst around its birthdays, although of course it didn't know anything about birthdays, and probably couldn't be blamed for doing it deliberately.

Since its birth, it had successfully fought off doses of strep throat, pinkeye, flu, and numerous colds. It had also mended a broken big toe so perfectly that only the slightest knobble of bone appeared under the skin when Martha bent it.

There was nothing remarkable about this body's past. It had gone through all the usual milestones, crawling, walking, talking, without too much fuss. And at sixteen, there was nothing very remarkable about its present. It mostly just got on with its job.

Lying in my hospital bed with all those read and unread books around me, I wondered once what it would be like if there was only one human body in the whole wide world. Surely it would be proclaimed as a wonder. A miracle. Such a richly functioning collection of tiny interlocking parts: and housing a human! Awesome. Mind boggling. UNESCO would name it an international treasure. They'd build a theme park around it, and guard it with an army.

But there isn't just one human body, there are billions. *So many of you,* Simon said.

Familiarity breeds contempt.

Did Martha feel contempt for her body? This thing she'd spent sixteen years living inside?

Children don't separate themselves from their bodies. When their bodies are working fine, they're not aware of them. When their bodies give them pain or discomfort – when they come off their scooters, or have pinkeye, or throw up – it isn't happening to their bodies, it's happening to *them.*

Martha snuggling up to Joan's body, deep in Joan's quilt. Martha being caught and swung by long-limbed Lionel.

Lots of kids are body-conscious before they ought to be, but Martha wasn't one of them. Growing up, she doesn't remember mirrors.

When you're a really young kid, what you're aware of more than anything is other people's bodies. *That man's fat!* you say loudly in a supermarket, just before your mum clouts you. And then, every so often, you get glimpses of other people's bodies that pull you up short. Your best friend's thin, mottled knees as she sits on the toilet. The hairs on your brother's back when he takes off his shirt. Your dad's ripped fingernail dripping blood as he tinkers with an engine. These sights are wonderful and shocking and strange – they're almost an epiphany – because they're a sudden realisation that there are other bodies, too, very different from yours, and other, very different souls that are living inside them.

These glimpses only last a moment, even though you'll never forget them. When the next moment arrives, you're oblivious again: one with your body, and with the rest of the world. But perhaps these glimpses, these flashes of realisation, are a way of preparing you for what's coming next.

What's coming next, of course, is mirrors, and Instagram, and always checking your wardrobe. It isn't just you any more, it's you and your body, and how you're going to clothe it and paint it and pierce it and tattoo it. Not a million miles different from Martha in Air, you and your body have separated.

Martha didn't get obsessed about how she presented her body to the world. She knows she was lucky, watching some of her classmates. And she knows she was unlucky, too, in a way. She was probably deficient. She probably didn't care enough. Still, there were a couple of boys who found her attractive, in spite of her not caring, and she took advantage of their liking of her body, however casually adorned it was.

She took advantage, once or twice, and her body responded. But Martha and her body were now two different things, and Martha stayed numb.

❖ ❖ ❖

It was Mark who tried to help her with puberty. Obviously he'd decided that Joan wasn't up to it. Martha was twelve years old.

"Hey, sis. I wanted to talk to you."

I want. Not, *I need.* This was when Mark still thought he could take control of what the world wanted to do to him.

Martha was sitting on her bed in her pyjamas. Mark didn't read to her any longer, but he still made sure he was around to kiss her goodnight.

"Have they told you at school about periods?"

He'd sat down on one corner of the bed, and clasped his big hands between his knees. His expression looked rueful, and concerned, and a little bit alarmed.

"Yes," Martha said.

"I just wanted to make sure you were okay. I mean, have you started?"

"No," Martha said.

"Well. When you do... Are you okay about buying tampons?"

"Yes," Martha said.

"Great. But if there's anything else you want to ask me. I mean, I'm here for you, little sis. You know you can ask me anything, don't you?"

"Thanks," Martha said.

Martha loves her brother wholeheartedly for trying to have this conversation. Martha had started to bleed six months before it happened, and her sock drawer was stuffed with Lil-Lets. Oh, but her brother had been wonderful. That great, unbroken, bear of a man.

Martha strips naked and looks at herself in the mirror. She sees a female body. Martha's body. No tattoos. No piercings below her ears. No threaded ladder of scars on her abdomen, either.

She knows about body dysmorphia, and assumes she doesn't have it. There isn't enough of an emotional reaction to have it. She doesn't have gender dysmorphia, either. When she looks at this body, Martha's got no objections to calling it a she. *It is what it is.*

She sees things about it that she's okay with, and things about it that could probably be smoother, or shapelier, or thinner. She knows there are plenty of ways in which she could look after it more. Get an electric toothbrush. Take up jogging. Cut down on the Doritos. But she's got no real intention of doing any of these things.

Martha strips naked and looks at herself in the mirror. Then she shrugs, and clothes it in pyjamas, and goes to bed, and forgets about it.

3

What body could Veronica possibly want? If she didn't want Martha's, *who's* body could she want? And what would happen to the soul that was inside this other body when Veronica took control of it?

We can be each other's angels, Veronica had said.

What the hell did she mean by *that?*

Martha was reeling from what Veronica had told her. Veronica was or wasn't a soul – she was more, or less, than a Being of Air – and she'd once been in Earth, with a body of her own. She'd had a different name. But she didn't have an angel, and how was *that* possible? And was any of it even true, or had Veronica been lying to her?

The words *Like you* kept repeating themselves to Martha.

I refused my body. I entered Air, and drifted.
I wouldn't submit. I raged against it.

Was it all just a clever story; a way Veronica had found of aligning herself with Martha, of trying to gain her sympathy? Martha didn't know, but it was definitely a possibility she had to guard herself against. Veronica had fascinated her since the moment Martha had first seen her. Sometimes it felt like Veronica was hypnotising her.

They were still in the park. The pair of school kids had wandered away, the boy with his arm angled over the girl's shoulders, the girl weeping silently. Veronica had ignored them as they went. Martha was glad. For a few moments, she'd been fearful for them.

Veronica was staring at her.

"If we go to your body," she said, "right now, I can show you how to get in."

Oh, God, thought Martha. She didn't want to go anywhere with Veronica, and least of all back to that intensive care unit. She ought to be looking for her brother. She ought to try to find Simon and plead with him to help her. Ready or not (and she knew she wasn't), she ought to be braving the upper reaches of Air in search of her angel. But did she have a choice? The thought of Veronica visiting her body without her was terrifying.

"Okay," she said.

They moved together. They were quite a long way above the hospital roof. The town spread itself around it, roads and buildings, cars and people.

"Wait," Veronica said. "I want to show you something."

"What?"

"Just wait. And look."

Martha held herself still. Air murmured past and through her, occasional flurries of it catching at her, edging her sideways.

"There," Veronica said, and pointed.

Martha tried to follow the line of Veronica's arm, and her gaze came to rest on something near the incinerator chimney. It was a disturbance; an eddy, like the pulling out of a bath plug. It was a funnel of Air, rising skywards; and then, Martha saw it pluck something into itself. The instant before, it was empty. The instant after, something new had filled it.

"What is it?" she said.

Martha was entranced. She tried to focus on it, but its form kept flickering and shifting. It was glowing gently, although she couldn't have said what colour it was.

"A soul that's left its body," said Veronica.

Could it be so? Was this what Simon and Veronica saw when they looked at Martha? *A rose. A feather. A flame.* But yes: all of these were true.

The soul began to drift towards them. It couldn't see them, Martha realised; and although she could look at it, she couldn't see *into* it. If this was a human soul, there was no way of telling the age or the gender of the body it had left behind. It was now quite close, and Martha felt how gorgeous it was. Like oil on water, it glimmered and altered.

Then, suddenly, it brightened. It flared like a

match. And slowly at first, but accelerating, and very soon too rapidly to follow, it rose straight up.

And was gone. The eddy of Air that had held it spun itself away into nothing.

Martha turned to Veronica, amazed and trembling; but Veronica was pointing somewhere else.

"And there," she said.

Another soul was rising, out towards the motorway. Even so distant, there was no mistaking what it was. Martha watched until it, too, had vanished into that other distance; and then, she spread her gaze over the town, and out towards the city, and saw more: rising like ghostly sky lanterns, or bubbles of Earth, and then gone.

Did so many die, she wondered?

And so many born, too.

A pestilence.

But the souls she saw were unspeakably beautiful.

"Why didn't I see them before?" she said.

"Because you didn't know how to look," answered Veronica.

"Why? Why have you shown me?"

Veronica widened her luminous eyes.

"To remind you how easy dying is. To remind you what you are, and how helpless you are, and how you got here. Leaving your body is child's play, human soul. It's only the flimsiest of miracles that ties you to Earth in the first place. Going back's going to be much, much harder."

Veronica grinned.

"Well? Are you ready to try it?"

4

I want to write that Martha's heart was in her mouth as she fell through the ceiling of the ICU with Veronica, but of course, her heart was just where it had always been, along with every other physical part of her. Martha's body had no visitors, this time. Martha wondered how often Joan and Mark came, and how long they stayed.

A nurse was cleaning it. Martha was astonished at the gentleness and care of the hands that held the sponge and lifted tubes and wires, and wiped the body's waxy skin, and afterwards tucked gown and bedclothes back into place. The nurse said something to her body, before he moved on to the next patient. Martha saw his lips move, but she had no idea what he might have said.

Veronica waited until the nurse had finished, then left Martha's side and floated down to the bed. She lay above Martha's body, head to head and chest to chest, just inches above it. Then she looked round and up, and beckoned with her eyes.

Martha went down to her. What else could she have done?

"Look," said Veronica. "It's clay. It's Earth, and nothing else. I can show you a way in. But you've got to promise me something."

"What," Martha said.

"You've got to promise to come out again. Once you've learnt how to do it, I need you to help *me* do it."

"What?" she repeated.

"I can't get into Earth without you, Martha Mud. I told you: you're the gate. You're the key."

"No," Martha said. "I don't know. I can't promise you anything. Whose body do you want? You still haven't told me."

"Don't worry, they won't miss it. I've already found one, and its soul's given up on it."

"How do you know?"

Veronica laughed.

"How did *you* know what your mother was thinking? I've already taught you *that!*"

Martha felt caught in a spell. She knew Veronica was bewitching her, but she felt powerless to break free of it.

"My angel," she said. "They told me I needed my angel."

"But you told your angel to go fuck itself, didn't you? They lied about your angel, Martha. *I* never had an angel. If you trust me, you'll be back inside your body. That's what you want, isn't it?"

"Yes."

"As long as you come out again. But leaving's easy, like I said. Now. Are you ready?"

"What do I do?" asked Martha.

Veronica explained, and Martha listened. I don't think I can try to repeat her explanation. I don't think I could make it make sense. But Veronica was right: human souls are the border between Air and Earth.

Thoughts, in Earth, become Air.

Martha, in Air, slipped quietly into Earth.

Together, she and her body started breathing.

Veronica had been wrong about it being hard. It was effortless. It was like jumping from a wall and being caught. It was like water molecules when the temperature drops, and they arrange themselves in ways they already know – complicated ways, but ways they've been practising since Earth first started – and because they remember how to do it, the water freezes.

Why hadn't Martha tried it before?

This was her body. It fit like a glove. Bones, and blood, and coiled intestines.

She waggled her tongue. She wriggled her fingers.

She was blind, however. Her eyes were closed, and Martha couldn't open them. And then she became aware of other things.

There was a pipe stuck in her throat, and a pipe in her stomach. There were drugs in her body that walled away pain. This pain was a dragon, a monster, that wanted to destroy her. And the drugs were dulling her. If she let them, they'd make her forget herself. If she didn't leave this body soon, she'd sink into sleep.

Quite suddenly it felt wrong for Martha to be there. It felt wrong in every way. Her body was in deep distress. It didn't want her: not as she was.

Come out! said a voice.

Martha fought to hear it.

Come out! You promised!

The voice echoed from somewhere above her. She was drowning, fathoms deep in a dark ocean, and falling further into deeper darkness with every second that passed.

She sank, and her body groaned with the weight of her.

Go now, or I will die, said her body.

Oh, but then...

Between these conflicting voices, and even as she fell, Martha started remembering. Her body called back memories to her. These memories were inside her body, and she couldn't escape them.

Martha remembered how she'd felt on Suicide Bridge.

5

At the beginning of the week, I gave my counsellor what I've written so far. I don't have a printer, so I put it on a memory stick and gave it to mum to print out at work. I know I haven't quite got to the end, but I wanted some kind of feedback.

It's been really difficult, typing this up. Trying to decide how best to tell it, even when it felt like it was basically untellable. Trying to choose my words. So before I go ahead and finish it, I need to know if Mary thinks I've been wasting my time. I need to know if she likes it.

Now it's Friday, and as I'm wheeled up the entrance ramp of the CAMHS building, I'm particularly nervous. Far more nervous than the first time I came here, when I was actually looking forward to telling my counsellor how much I didn't need her services. You hear writers talk about their books being their children. I've never had children, and I don't know, now, if I even can, but if this is how it feels – all-consuming possessiveness, and heart-fluttering anxiety about putting them into the care of anyone else – then

I'm not sure I want to try it.

I don't have to wait long in reception before I'm called. Mary's always punctual.

My arms are getting stronger, slowly, and I can get myself down the corridor to her office without any help. She's already there as I approach, holding the door open for me.

"Good morning, Martha," she says with a smile. "How are you today?"

Round the side of her, I can see her desk. My manuscript's sitting on top of it.

"I'm okay," I say. "Although my neck's been aching. I'm seeing my physio tomorrow, but I'm beginning to think he's a sadist."

Mary laughs. She sits in her chair. Smoothes her skirt and adjusts her glasses. Glances at the clock. Then looks at me levelly.

All her tiny rituals.

"So," she says. "I've been reading your book."

"What do you think?" I ask her.

I'm trying to sound nonchalant. I've been trying as well to find something in her eyes that might betray her opinion of it, but for the moment, Mary's in fine professional form, and nothing shows.

In fact, she's right at the top of her game. She answers my question with a question.

"How did it feel, writing it all down?"

"Exhausting," I say.

"Well, it's a lot of paper you've filled. Although I can see it isn't quite finished. I hope you're going to get round to writing the rest of it?"

"I can hardly stop now," I say.

Mary laughs again.

"Thank you for you giving it to me, Martha. I appreciate how much effort you've put into it."

Except now I'm getting impatient.

"Yes," I say, "but what did you *think* of it?"

"What did *I* think? Well. I'm impressed with your vocabulary. I must admit I had to look up anemology."

"Dictionaries," I say. "They're awesome. And a thesaurus comes in handy, too."

"I wasn't sure about all those capital letters, though. Air. Earth. Being. They looked a bit odd, on the page."

"They looked a bit odd in real life as well," I say. "I tried losing the capital letters. But that just looked wrong."

"Okay," said Mary. "I trust you. Anyway, it's impressive. I don't doubt you'll fly through your English GCSE."

"Thanks," I say.

I jumped at the start of Year 11; by now, I've missed more than a whole year of school. GCSEs are going to be my next big adventure, I'm guessing.

After another few moments of me waiting, I say:

"But you still haven't really told me anything. You still haven't told me what you think of the actual story."

Mary raises her eyebrows.

"It's...*intense*," she says. "There's no let-up, is there?"

"No. No, there wasn't," I say.

And now, my counsellor clamps her lips together, and closes her eyes. She takes a breath. I wonder what she's thinking. Then she opens her eyes again, and looks straight at me. Her face is a hundred different things. Amused. Bewildered. Sceptical. Burningly curious. I'm not sure how one human face can cram in so many different emotions, but somehow, Mary's does.

"Do you know, Martha," she says, "I've been in this business for a good many years, and although I've had every kind of client you could imagine, I can honestly say there's been no-one quite like you."

She smiles at me. In spite of all the other things I can see in her face, it's a warm, self-deprecating smile, and I can't help but smile back.

"You've written about *us*," she says. "These sessions."

I was waiting for this.

"Yes," I say. "I'm sorry. It felt like it was part of the story. And writing about them helped me make sense of them."

"You didn't mince your words, did you? Is that how you see me, Martha?"

"Yes," I say.

Mary grins and rolls her eyes.

"You know, there's a school of therapy where

the therapist is supposed to learn as much about themselves as they learn about their client. The therapy's supposed to be mutual. Maybe it's something I should look into."

"Maybe," I say. "But what about the rest of it? The stuff about Air? Did I manage to make what happened any clearer?"

"Yes," says Mary. "Yes, your story's clearer. It's much clearer. It's actually helped me a lot."

Mary stops, and considers. I can see there's lots she wants to say, but she isn't sure where to begin.

"Why have you called me 'Mary'?"

"Mary was the name of my teacher. The teacher from New Zealand, in Junior School."

"Oh," says Mary. And then, remembering: *"Oh... Okay."*

She takes a moment to digest this.

"And why have you got me calling you 'Martha' when you're describing these sessions? I think I'm beginning to understand why you've changed your name when you talk about what happened to you. But now you're... *back*...."

"I know," I say. "But I didn't know how else to write it. I'm no longer Martha Mud. I'm a different Martha, now. Maybe I'm Martha Miraculous. Maybe I'm Martha Re-imagined."

"Okay!"

This time, Mary's laugh sounds entirely genuine. She's actually beginning to enjoy herself, and it's surprising her.

"So you've got to where Veronica tried to get you back into your body," she says. "And your body rejected you."

"Yes," I say. "That was only fair, wasn't it, after *I'd* rejected *it.* I got what I deserved."

"And you've still got the hardest part to write. If you're going to finish it."

"It's all been hard," I say. "But, yes. Okay. I know what you mean."

Mary looks at me. This is the most straight-forward, the most human, I've ever seen her.

"Your story's really shaken me up, Martha," she says. "I don't know whether to believe it. I don't know how I *can* believe it. It's such a strange mix of…"

"What?" I say.

"Of stuff that really happened to you. Bits of your past. Of what's true, and what isn't. Of what *can't* be true."

But I don't want to have this argument again, so I say:

"It's a mix of Earth and Air. Just like us."

"That's pretty cryptic, Martha."

"I know," I say.

I know as well that there are all sorts of ways I've been able to verify my experiences in Air, subjectively, but that none of them would convince my counsellor. How else could I have known about Timpson's Solicitors, lying unconscious in that hospital? How else could I have known about Mark? But Mary's still free to believe that I found out about these things *after* I woke up, and then wove them into my own contrived little fairy-tale.

Mary shakes her head. She doesn't want to rehash this argument, either.

"I'm sorry," she says. "You've convinced me that you think all this really happened to you, and that ought to be enough."

But now I've thought of a way out for her. The idea makes me smile.

"Why don't you just assume it *isn't* true?" I say.

"Excuse me?"

"Assume I'm making it all up. Does my story tell you what you need to know about me, as my counsellor? Does it explain how I'm a different person to the Martha who jumped?"

"Yes," says Mary. "Yes, it does explain it." She's grinning again. "Although it wouldn't explain why you're such a compulsive liar."

"Fiction is the lie through which we tell the truth. That's a quote. A 20th Century French writer called Albert Camus. I told you I've been reading a lot lately."

Mary looks hard at me.

"Martha, are you telling me now you *did* make it up?"

"No," I say.

There are lots of words that human beings have somehow managed to turn on their heads, so that the meanings we give to them now are the exact opposite of the meanings we gave them originally. These words map the paradigm shifts we've lived through, without most of us apparently taking much notice. *Myth* is one of them. If today we say that something's a myth, we mean it probably isn't real. It's made up. It's just a story. But myths have been the way we've tried to tell truths about the world since the dawn of time.

Subjective and *objective* are two more words that we've flipped upside down. Actually, they literally just exchanged definitions, so that if someone four hundred years ago wanted to describe something that was true for everyone, that was externally verifiable, they'd call it *subjective,* and if it was only true inside someone's head, they'd call it *objective,* which of course is the exact reverse of what we'd do today. But still it makes you wonder. I mean, if these meanings were switched with such apparent ease, then is the enormous distinction we make between them actually all that important?

I know Mary would love to be able to prove the reality of my story, one way or the other. But *I* know it's true. It's true for *me.* Why does it have to be true – at least, true in the same way – for anyone else?

"So you're happy I wrote it," I say. "You think it's okay."

I want to get back to what Mary thinks of my book, only now I'm afraid I'm sounding too needy.

"Yes," says Mary. "And thank you, again.

It's been a big help. And I'm looking forward to reading the rest of it."

"Okay," I say.

There's a slightly awkward silence. We can both feel that *It's been a big help* is hardly literary criticism. But really, I don't know what else I'd been expecting. Do authors always experience this when they send their books out into the world? Do any of them ever find that perfect reader: the one they've been unknowingly writing for all along; the one who's been watching over their shoulder through the whole difficult process; the one who's been willing them to pick out those exact words – just those – that this reader needed to hear?

"Will you do something for me?" Mary asks.

"What?"

"When you come to write the bit you keep putting off. The bit I can see you keep circling around. The bit that ties the whole thing together. Will you write it in the first person? Will you write it as *you*, Martha?"

"I don't know," I say.

"Well, think about it. See if it makes sense to you."

"Okay," I say.

Well, I have thought about it. I've thought an awful lot about it. And yes, it does make sense.

Thank you, Mary.

My counsellor might not be my book's perfect reader, but maybe she's *my* perfect reader.

What does it take to read a person?

Compassion, and careful attention, and a willingness to believe in them.

A willingness, just the same, to call them out when we believe that they're lying.

6

Martha Mud's body made Martha remember how she'd felt on Suicide Bridge. It poured these memories into her, and she couldn't escape them.

These were the memories.

I'm not sure what I was thinking about as I made my way up that hill. I'd like to say I had a premonition; a sense that the world was about to go up in smoke. But I didn't.

Mark had never been particularly communicative, and even less in the last few months, so it was unlike him to be so direct. Normally he'd be jokey, and ask me something about myself whilst managing to steer our conversations away from anything about him. But it was obvious that that *We* in his text was really an *I*.

I need to talk.

Well, never before: not once. What had changed?

So yes, I was curious. And I was happy that

Mark wanted to see me. But I was also just happy to be out of school, and happy to have the late summer sunshine on my face, and a fresh little wind cooling the blisters on my fingers.

I stepped out onto the bridge and walked to the middle. I looked through the railings.

"Mark!" I said. "What the hell are you doing? That's stupidly dangerous!"

My brother didn't reply. He didn't even turn round to look at me. All I could see was the back of his head, and the ground all those meters below him.

"Mark?"

And then I knew. Sometimes, you just know things. Panic nearly shook me to pieces. I looked up and down the cycle path, but there was no-one around. What should I do? I had my phone in my school bag. Should I call 999?

"I can't do this any more, sis," my brother said.

"Wait. Just wait. I'm coming down."

I'd always known how to get through the barbed wire and climb out along the bridge. I'd seen kids camped out on that ledge before, smoking spliffs and horsing around on the railings. I'd followed the route with my mind's eye a dozen times, safe in the knowledge that I'd never be dumb enough to actually do it. Well, now I was actually doing it. I ripped my jacket on the barbed wire. I felt it snag, and just pulled my way through. Then I was swinging in the wind with nothing to catch me, hauling myself along towards my brother, sheer blind terror cramping my fingers round the cold metal bars.

My feet found the ledge, and I tried to suck myself into the side of the bridge as I twisted myself round to sit on it. I've never been good with heights, and we were such a long, long way above those rocks.

Mark still wouldn't look at me. He was just staring down between his knees. His face looked like it had been punched.

Once I was next to him, I don't know exactly what we said to each other. For a little while, I don't think we said anything at all. I've been writing this story all along with speech marks, as if the words you're reading are exactly the words that everyone in it said; but of course, they aren't. I have to recreate it. I have to re-imagine. The words that were really said, by Martha, by Mark, by Simon, by Mary: those words are gone.

"Tell me what's happened," I said.

Mark told me.

What would you do, if your only brother told you that story? How would you feel? I can't ever know, and neither can you.

I felt like my life was ending. No, really. Mark was my rock. He was my angel. The idea of him happy, and strong, and coping, was what protected me from everything that made me miserable, and weak, and unable to carry on. If the world was too much for Mark to handle, what hope did I have?

This is hard to admit, but it's true: as I listened to his story, all I could think of was my own story. Joan absent, and Lionel absent, and every day empty, and just something to be survived.

"I'm sorry, sis," Mark said. "I'm so sorry. I think I'm going."

"No," I said. "You can't. If you go, I'll follow you."

I was convinced Mark meant it. I didn't doubt for one moment he was ready to jump. When I saw him in the hospital, I decided that I'd probably been wrong; but I still don't know this for an absolute fact. What would have happened if I'd just kept talking? Maybe I'd have been able to persuade him back onto the cycle path. Maybe someone else would have come along and helped us. Maybe I'd have dialled the Samaritans. There are so many questions no-one will ever know the answer to.

I think now that I probably failed my brother, when I thought I was saving him. At the moment of my brother's greatest need, maybe I just ended up being selfish. But maybe you think you *can* answer that one, Mary.

Maybe I can, too.

"Why did you jump, Martha?"

Mary isn't often this blunt, and it takes me by

surprise.

"I jumped to stop my brother jumping," I tell her.

"No. I'm sorry, Martha. That doesn't add up. If you love someone who's hanging off a bridge, you try to talk them out of it. You call the emergency services. You might panic. But you don't do *that.*"

"I jumped because I wanted to," I say. "I jumped because hearing Mark tell me how worthless his life had become made me see how worthless mine was, too.

"I committed suicide on Suicide Bridge."

I climbed onto him. I threw my legs over his broad knees, and gripped his face. I was in tears by then. Just endless tears.

"This is wrong," I said. "Life is wrong."

I don't know what I said.

Then I pushed myself away from him, and Mark was too amazed to be able to stop me.

So Martha Mud fell backwards from Suicide Bridge, and fell, and fell.

7

What do you do when you honestly feel your life isn't worth living? When you look back at your past, and all you can see is a succession of disappointments that just keep adding up, like a column of negative numbers in a maths sum, until the *now* they've brought you to is a big fat zero?

I can rationalise about it, after the event. I can say jumping was a blind and stupid thing to do. I could list a dozen different things I *might* have done that would have been far cleverer. But that was a different me on that bridge, and she was overwhelmed with what she was feeling.

Which, of course, is just another rationalisation...

This book's been trying to tell you there are three Marthas in my story. The Martha who got sidetracked by her own despair and jumped. The Martha who's typing this, right now – Martha Miraculous, or whatever you want to call her – the Martha who came back again. And the Martha who got a second chance; who even after she died, got to see what she'd done to the people who still cared about her; who discovered that dying wasn't an exit, it was just more living, with all the same terrors and dashed hopes and difficult decisions that she'd wanted to get away from.

Three Marthas...

In all honesty, though, there's only one Martha Mud: there always has been.

But you already knew that, dear reader, didn't you?

8

You promised! yelled Veronica.

It was just the opposite of what Veronica had told her. Getting in had been easy; getting out again was exquisitely difficult.

Martha's consciousness fought its way up through those dark, druggy waters, and then found itself on the border. Here was her mangled body, where she was. Out there, somewhere else, was the place Veronica's voice was coming from. But her flesh felt so heavy.

Come out! Come out!

Her flesh was dragging her down, but at the same time, it couldn't bear her being there. *Go now, or I'll die,* it said. Every nerve and muscle and organ and cavity was drenched with the despair she'd experienced on Suicide Bridge. *I'm not ready,* said her body. You're *not ready.*

I can't leave, Martha said, having no idea what or who she was speaking to. *I don't know how.*

Like this, you idiot! said Veronica. *Stop holding onto it! Just let go!*

Could she?

One moment, it seemed worse than impossible; the next, like a bubble popping on the surface of herself, Martha sprang back into Air again.

Her body lay below her. She was just as she had been, nothing but a soul: weightless, and formless, and thin.

She turned on Veronica.

"That was wrong," she said. "That was worse than listening to my mother. I shouldn't have done it. My body didn't want me."

"Why?" said Veronica.

"I don't know! It has to be what Simon said. I need a shape! I need my angel!"

Veronica laughed.

"Simon understands Air, but he doesn't know a thing about Earth. Or angels, for that matter. The point is, you did it. I told you you could, and you did. So who was right?"

"No," said Martha. "No, Veronica. There was something missing. My body couldn't cope."

"You went back into Earth. I've shown you the way in. That was my part of the bargain, and now it's your turn. Now *you're* going to help *me* do it."

What? A bargain? Was that what it had been? Martha saw suddenly that yes, it was. How could she have been so stupid? Veronica had used Martha's desire and curiosity as bait for a trap, just as she'd done when Martha wanted to find Lionel. Well, Martha's curiosity had certainly been satisfied. She'd wanted to know if returning to her body was possible, if taking a shortcut was possible, and she'd discovered that no, it really wasn't, despite what Veronica had claimed. But now she was in Air again, and Veronica wanted payment for her services.

Had Martha imagined she'd try to break her promise, never mind that she'd only made it tacitly? Had she imagined she'd try to stay in Earth once she got there?

Yes. She had.

"I don't know how to help," she said. "I don't think I can."

"You don't need to know," said Veronica. "Come with me. We're going somewhere."

Following Veronica through Air wasn't exactly challenging. Veronica left a wake behind her as she moved; an agitation; a churning of the element. Where Simon had flown lightly like a skater over ice, Veronica tore great chunks out of it. She was growing monstrous, Martha realised. Air had become too insubstantial for her, or her name too weighty for her.

They halted. They'd arrived, wherever it was. Veronica's hair twined around her ankles as she turned to face Martha. The daffodil of her dress had changed to a bruised ruby-red. Her eyes were two amethysts, crystalline and cold.

"Soon a body will come," she said. "And you're going to get me inside it."

Martha looked around her. They were in a bedroom. It was small and bare and dirty. A mattress lay on the floor under a curtainless window, and a TV sat in the opposite corner. There wasn't much else. Scattered clothes, and empty beer cans, and tousled bedding. A laptop on a battered little table, and next to it an unwashed plate and coffee cup.

Oh, God, thought Martha. Where are we? Who does this belong to?

"Veronica, what are you doing?" she said. "You can't just steal a body. This is bad! This is evil!"

"I already told you. He doesn't want it. He's already in the process of throwing it away. If you pick something up off the floor, you can't call it stealing."

"He?"

"I don't care what sex it is. It's young and strong. I was a woman in Earth, once upon a time. The world had never known such youth and strength as I had then. What do you see when you look at me now?"

"A skinny little girl," said Martha.

Veronica grimaced.

"I'm sick of Air. It's made me sick. It's made me nothing. I've been stuck in Air for far too long."

Martha was beginning to panic. This room stank of something desperate that made her want to bolt. Flashes of what her body had told her kept coming back to her: what she had done to it, and why she had done it. The room, and these flashes, seemed part of one another.

In Earth, the door of the room opened, and someone entered.

It was Mark.

Martha's first thought wasn't surprise, it was recognition. Of course it was Mark. It couldn't have been anyone else. And for all Simon's warnings, she hadn't grasped the truth about Veronica till now. She'd tried to excuse her, and understand her, and make deals with her, but all this child had ever intended was to bring her pain and tear her down.

"No," she said. "Not my brother."

"Yes," replied Veronica. "If you're going to do what we agreed, there's no-one else."

Mark sat down on the mattress. He looked the same as he'd looked in the hospital. He was absent. His body might as well have been hijacked already, because Mark wasn't there.

He reached under his pillow and took something out. It was wrapped in plastic. Then he got busy with other things, and Martha saw at once what he was doing, and saw where his absence had dragged him to. This was Mark's own jump from Suicide Bridge; his own means of expressing and refusing the agony life was causing him.

Veronica was rapt.

"I've been watching him," she murmured. "I've been watching what it does to him. It blurs the boundary. You can see what's tying him to his body start to melt."

Martha's heart was breaking. Her big, strong brother. This was worse than the bridge; worse than the intensive care ward.

"Soon," said Veronica, "he'll be ready. It doesn't take long. When I tell you to, you've got to talk to him. But you've got to be quick, because if we don't time it right, he won't be able to hear you."

"Talk to him?" said Martha.

"Tell him to come out. Tell him to let go. You know exactly how it's done, because you just did it yourself."

"What?"

Veronica rounded on her.

"Listen! You're going to do this because you promised! And you're also going to do this because you know it's the best thing for him. It's the only thing for him. Look at him. He's lost. He's given up."

"No," Martha said.

"Think about it. You can be together. You can show him Air. You can go and look for each other's angels for all I care. But he'll be *happier*. You'll be happier."

"No."

"Yes! Why do you think you're here, Martha Mud? You jumped to stop him throwing himself away, but you failed. You ruined your body on those rocks for nothing, because now he's eating himself up with guilt about what you did. He's destroying himself because of *you,* Martha. Look at him!"

Martha looked, and understood very clearly that Veronica was simply stating a fact.

"This is your chance to really save him. This is your only chance. You can make amends, but you've got to do it now. Help him, Martha. Help him *out.*"

Mark had slumped back onto the mattress, paraphernalia strewed around him. His eyes were closing in on themselves, his jaw going slack.

Veronica started speaking very quickly. Her words felt like bullets from a chain gun.

"Do it soon. He's ready. If you don't do it now, you won't get another opportunity. I'll be gone. You won't ever see me again. I certainly won't ever be coming back *here,* but you will, Martha Mud. If you're really too scared to go back into your body – if you're too scared to do *this!* – then this place will draw you like a magnet. Your soul won't waste away drifting, it will waste away here, in this room, watching your brother suffer. The knowledge that you're too weak to save him will shred you into bits."

Martha looked around at Mark's dismal surroundings, the dirt, the drab walls, and saw that if Veronica was right about everything else she'd just told her, she was right about this, too:

that's exactly what Martha would do. There'd be no shape for her. There'd be no angel.

She turned away from her brother; away from Veronica. She wanted to flee, but knew she couldn't. Desperately, she tried to wriggle out of this last, unspeakably cruel snare Veronica had set for her. She tried to sift through Veronica's words to find a hole in her logic; to find something she'd said that might not be the truth.

Mark wanted an end to his life. There might have been doubt about that on Suicide Bridge, but there was no doubt now. What he was doing to his body was exactly what his boyfriend had done to *his* body, and Mark had tried so hard to rescue him from it. *I'm sorry, sis. I think I'm going.* That's what Mark had told her. But now, he really was.

Help him, Veronica was saying; and yes, Martha realised that it was perfectly possible. She could push herself down into that subtle, silken web between Air and Earth and talk to him, just as she'd talked to her mother. She could straddle the gap, and show him the way out – *Just let go!* – and Mark would be free of everything that was hurting him.

Then, they'd be together. They'd be together in Air, just as Veronica had said.

Imagining this, for an instant, Martha was overwhelmed by her own loneliness. Simon had left her, and there wasn't anyone else. She remembered those other human souls she'd seen rising: little motes of potential companionship that weren't even aware of her, that were lost to her almost in the instant they showed themselves.

To have her brother with her! To try to make shapes for each other. And yes, whether or not Veronica even believed that they could: to go together in search of their angels...

Of course we can lie, Simon had told her.

How was Veronica lying to her?

Veronica would get what she wanted. She'd have Mark's body: the bear, the mountain, however strung out. What did it matter what she chose to do with it? Mark wouldn't care. Mark had no use for it.

"*Now,* Martha."

Veronica had shoved herself close. Her eyes burned hard and bright.

"Do you love him, or don't you? You have to decide!"

Yes, Martha loved him. Of course she loved him. She'd loved him all through her childhood. She loved him right now. She'd loved him on the bridge.

Suddenly, more words of Veronica's came back to her.

You jumped to save him, but you failed.

Was this true?

You jumped to save him.

And the realisation that came to her now was really and truly like a lightning flash. No, she hadn't jumped to save him. She'd jumped for herself. She'd jumped to show him that *she* was suffering, too, and that her suffering was more unbearable than his, or why hadn't he already done it? Why had he summoned her to that bridge, and laid all his shit on his sixteen year old half-sister, and then expected her to rescue him from it?

And then Martha saw with absolute certainty that every choice she'd made in Air had been nothing but self-centred. She'd kept Simon close to her, and named him, even though she could see it was destroying him. She'd named Veronica just so that she could find her father; and wanting to find Lionel in the first place was selfish, when he clearly didn't want to be found.

Refusing her body. Refusing her angel.

All of it.

And now this?

"I committed suicide on Suicide Bridge," Martha said.

That's what I told you, Mary, wasn't it?

And it was true. It was the truest thing I ever said to you.

Martha turned to Veronica.

"I'm not going to help you," Martha said. "But I am going to try my best to help my brother. I can't do it in Air. I can't do it as I am. But I am going to do it."

Certain it was the right thing to do next, Martha moved.

PART SIX

1

She moved, and felt at once that something was different. *She* was different. Air opened up for her. The doors of Air swung wide for her, pulled by invisible hands. She was royalty, and Air bowed down to her.

She didn't know what place she came to, but wherever it was, the Being she'd called Simon was waiting for her.

He was just as radiant as when she'd last seen him. She stopped, afraid to go too near to him, dazzled, and glad.

Simon grinned at her.

"You triumphed. You wrestled the monster," he said.

"Yes," Martha said. "I guess I must have

done."

"Do you know you have a shape? But of course you know. I can't imagine you don't feel it."

"I feel something," Martha said. "But what do you see?"

Simon told her what he saw, and Martha recognised the truth of what he said to her.

Simon kept grinning, and Martha hung in Air, quietly bursting: sunning herself in this Being's regard.

"What will you do next?" he asked.

"I'll go up. I'll call my angel."

"Even now, it might not hear you. I hope it does, but I'm not qualified to make you promises."

"Simon, you've given the best advice, the kindest and wisest advice, that I could have wished for. You've been my friend when I didn't have anyone else. I know my angel's going to hear me. I'm going to make it hear me."

Simon bowed his head, and his light dimmed a little because of her.

"Will you go now? Are you ready?"

"Nearly," Martha said. "First I need to go somewhere else."

She was back above wide, breaking waves, looking down at the cottage on the beachfront. The sky was wild with clouds, and a wind that Martha couldn't feel rushed in from the sea, skimming foam from the water, flattening grasses at the roadside.

A man was walking his dog along the sand towards her. He stepped up onto the road, and crossed it. He pushed open the red door of the cottage, and the dog tumbled in. The man went in too, and closed the door behind him.

This man wasn't Martha's father.

She'd been intending to go down into the cottage, but now she saw she didn't need to, because she was quite certain of who the man was. This was Veronica's final piece of trickery, but if it had been intended to hurt her, Martha right now felt the opposite. And realising this, she sensed her shape thickening and crystallizing around her: who knew that the process hadn't yet finished? Perhaps, she thought wonderingly, it had only just started.

After a little while, smoke pushed its way out of the chimney and got sucked away by the wind. On this chilly Irish morning, her Uncle Liam had started a fire.

2

I've let Mary read the last little bit of this book. Now she's seen everything except what I'm typing now.

"But what about the rest of it?" she says, when I'm next in to see her.

She looks disappointed.

"I don't know," I say. "I tried to write it. But it just didn't feel like it worked. Honestly, Mary, I think it's better as it is."

"But calling your angel, and what you said to each other, and getting back into your body…"

"I never told you what we said to each other."

"No. No, you didn't."

Poor Mary. She'd been so curious.

I went up into the gale, and my shape held me safe. I out-faced the dragon. I went further, into Water, into Fire, but the words to describe what I found there aren't in any dictionary I've ever come across. And when I called my angel, my angel answered.

My angel answered.

When I told Mary I've tried to write this part

of my story, what I meant was, I stared at a blank page for a long, long time, and smiled.

The words I said to my angel, and the words it said to me, are private. But when I saw it, I knew straight away that all the questions I'd wanted to ask it didn't need asking.

It took me back to that body in the ICU, and holding my hand as I did it, in I climbed. My body started breathing. We started breathing. We reached an understanding.

Maybe we just agreed to put up with each other.

Martha Mud had been changing ever since she went up into Air, but now she was back in the Earth of her body, she had to learn how to bring all those changes with her, and that was hard.

Of course, this body has changed too, and that hasn't made the learning any easier. It certainly isn't the same body as the one I threw away! It's older, for one thing. It was lying there on its own in the hospital for months. Its legs don't work any more, they probably never will, and it gets a thousand pains and headaches that it never used to get. It lets me know daily that taking it for granted is no longer an option, and that for better or worse – for now, anyway – we're in this together. I realise I can't ever get back into Air again. Not until my body and I agree it's the right time for me to go.

Not surprisingly, the life I'm living now isn't the same life I threw away, either. I've got my mum back, because she's got herself back. We're both starting to get Mark back, although that's taken a long while. He's moved in with us, out of that horrible bedsit, and he's off the drugs. My mum ended up paying to put him into rehab, even though it left her short trying to pay for all the extra things I need now I'm out of hospital, but I wouldn't let her say no.

I sit with him at night, quite often. We don't say much, but it feels like we don't need to. Sometimes, I read to him, and then he reads to me. Bedtime stories. It's a nice little ritual: speaking other people's words to each other. One day soon, I'm hoping we'll discover how to speak our own words as well.

Oh, and I've got my Uncle Liam too, because writing to him was one of the first things I did when I was able to hold a biro. His reply came almost by return of post. Do you know what he said? *I had a feeling you were going to get in touch again.*

How did he know?

But if there's one thing Air has taught me, it's to not be surprised at the miraculous. To start expecting the miraculous. And believe it or not, the more you expect it, you more it starts happening to you.

Liam's coming for a visit in the summer. When we finally get it together to go and visit him, I already know what his house is going to look like. (Actually, I've cheated, and Google Earthed his address. Hardly front page news, but it's just the same as I remember it.)

Liam's a million miles better than Lionel, because I'm pretty sure Liam actually cares. My desire to find Lionel has completely evaporated.

But anyway, I was describing my last visit to my counsellor, wasn't I? As a matter of fact, it really is my last visit. If I've got the right word for it, I'm being discharged.

Mary says:

"Well, it's your book, Martha, obviously. And if that's how you want to finish it…"

I shrug at her. There's nothing to finish, and everything to begin.

"Have you thought about showing this story to anyone else?" Mary asks.

"No," I say. This question's thrown me, and I try to imagine. "I could show it my mum," I say. "I don't know what she'd make of it."

"What about your brother?"

"Oh, God, no! There's no way he's ready for it."

"Your brother isn't ready?" says Mary. "Or you aren't ready?"

I feel a violent urge to argue with this, just briefly, and then I have to smile. Sometimes, sitting here with Mary, I think I forget that she's supposed to be my counsellor; but Mary never forgets. She's really very good at what she does. She's rather brilliant, actually.

"I don't know," I say.

Rather lamely, as usual.

"It might help him," says Mary. "It might help both of you."

And, yes. It might.

"Of course, you could always try and get it published. Other people might want to read it."

Would they? Really? This isn't something I'd considered.

"What would I call it?" I say.

"I've no idea," laughs Mary. "Martha Mud and the Monster. Martha's Adventures in Air. A Book To Read If You Feel Life Isn't Worth Living."

I know my counsellor was joking, but to be honest, I kind of like that last title. It's quirky, and dumb, and actually pretty accurate.

Dear reader…

Well, all along I'd been assuming you were Mary, and now, I'm not so sure!

I think I am going to try and get this book published. I've tidied it up, as much as my hugely messy story *can* be tidied up. And I'm going to go back and add a couple of things, bearing in mind that you might not be the person I thought you were.

After that, all I've got to do is sign it.

ABOUT THE AUTHOR

Martha Mud

 Martha is still living; for now, in a house in a small town near London, England, that she's sharing with her mum. Her brother moved out a little while ago. He's probably doing better than either of us.

Martha passed her GCSEs. She's been looking at colleges. But there's no rush.

Printed in Great Britain
by Amazon